RUNNER

RUNNER

CARL DEUKER

Houghton Mifflin Company
Boston 2005

The author would like to thank the editor of this book,
Ann Rider, for her advice and encouragement.

Text copyright © 2005 by Carl Deuker

www.houghtonmifflinbooks.com

The text of this book is set in 11-point Scala.

Library of Congress Cataloging-in-Publication Data
Deuker, Carl.
Runner / by Carl Deuker.
p.   cm.
Summary: Living with his alcoholic father on a broken-down sailboat on Puget Sound has been
hard on seventeen-year-old Chance Taylor, but when his love of running leads to a high-paying job,
he quickly learns that the money is not worth the risk.
ISBN 0-618-54298-1
[1. Smuggling—Fiction. 2. Alcoholism—Fiction. 3. Single-parent families—Fiction. 4. Poverty—
Fiction. 5. Terrorism—Fiction. 6. Puget Sound (Wash.)—Fiction.] I. Title.
PZ7.D493Ru 2005   [Fic]—dc22   2004015781

ISBN-13: 978-0618-54298-7

Manufactured in the United States of America
MP 10 9 8 7 6 5 4 3 2 1

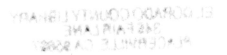

FOR ANNE AND MARIAN

PART ONE

CHAPTER ONE

I've read about kids who hate their parents for being alcoholics. I've never understood that. It'd be like hating a wounded animal for being wounded, which makes no sense at all. Lots of times my dad made me mad, lots of times he left me alone and lonely, but I never once hated him, not even when he was at his rock-bottom worst, not even when I thought he was both a coward and a drunk.

Nobody would ever call him a coward now, not with the way things ended. But talking about how things ended makes no sense without understanding how it all began. The hard part is knowing where to start. The stuff with my mother happened when I was in sixth grade, and my father got booted out of the army a couple of years before that. But those things are hazy to me. What's completely clear is this school year, beginning with September 11, the anniversary of the terrorist attacks on the World Trade Center and the Pentagon.

School is always different on September 11. This year, instead of going straight to class, we had an assembly first period. The choir sang patriotic songs, the principal gave a speech, the marching band played *The Star-Spangled Banner*. In every class—even math class—teachers led boring discussions. Kids around me took turns talking about terrorism, and Iraq, and Osama bin Laden, and al-Qaida. It seemed like everybody had an opinion about something.

Everybody but me. I didn't say a word in any of my morning classes; I just sat in the back and kept my mouth closed. But that was nothing new; it's what I'd been doing from the first day I entered Lincoln High. What I'd been doing from middle school, even. I took whatever classes the counselors gave me, did whatever schoolwork I had to do to get a passing grade, and disappeared from campus as soon as the final bell rang. I was one of the ghost-walkers in school.

My last class was World Issues with Mr. Arnold. The first time I saw Arnold, I thought I was looking at my dad's long-lost twin brother. They're both in their forties; they're both tall and thin; they both have deep-set brown eyes and graying beards.

But then I looked closer, and I saw all the differences. Arnold probably works out in the gym seven days a week. His clothes are always clean; his hair and beard are always neatly trimmed. My dad has long straggly hair and a stubbly beard. His clothes are as dirty as his hair, and he's got the raspy voice of a smoker and the blotchy skin of a drunk. The only exercise he gets is walking to the Sloop Tavern, and he doesn't even do that much. Most days he just lies around the broken-down

4

sailboat that we live on, drinking and smoking and reading the sports page over and over.

After I found my spot in the back of Arnold's classroom that day, I looked out the window. That wasn't new, but the flock of starlings that were attacking the lawn was. Their beaks would hammer down into the grass, and then they would gobble up whatever bug or worm they'd grabbed. They knew what they wanted, and they got it.

Arnold pushed the classroom door open just as the bell rang. Behind him was some guy who didn't look much older than me. His face was bright and shiny, and he was wearing a crisply pressed army uniform. As soon as I saw him, I knew what was coming: a long talk about how rewarding it was to be in the army, serving America and defending freedom. I looked back at the birds.

One really good thing about Arnold is that he leaves you alone. You look out the window, it's OK with him, just so long as you don't bother other kids. So I planned on looking out the window for fifty-five minutes before finally going home.

At first, Arnold's voice was like background noise. He was rattling on about how our guest was a recent graduate of Lincoln High, how a few of us might remember him, how brave and courageous he was. "So please, ladies and gentlemen, let's give our attention to Mr. Brent Miller."

CHAPTER TWO

Brent Miller.

My eyes turned back to the front of the class. I looked, and then looked again. The last time I'd seen Miller, he had green-tipped hair, wore ripped pants that hung down to his thighs, and was drinking wine and smoking dope at Salmon Bay Park with a bunch of guys who looked just like him.

Miller had been a senior at Lincoln High when I'd entered as a freshman, but I'd known him before that, known him and hated him. His dad was a vet of the first Gulf War just like my dad, and his dad was a drunk, just like mine. The two of them had hung out at the same taverns along Ballard Avenue.

Sometimes, Miller and I would be stuck together in his dad's crummy apartment or on my dad's smelly sailboat while our fathers drank themselves into stupors. It didn't happen often—every couple months or so—but once would have been one time too many. Brent and I would spend the hours glaring at each other.

A few weeks before I started at Lincoln High, Miller's dad and my dad got into some sort of shouting match at the Sunset Tavern. The bartender threw them both out, and on the sidewalk the shouting turned into a brawl. My dad ended up in jail for a couple of days; Miller's dad ended up at Harborview Hospital for the same amount of time. "I kicked his ass good," my dad told me when he got out.

Once school started, Miller made me pay. Every chance he got, he'd shove me up against the lockers and squeeze my face with his fat hand, putting on a big show for his friends. "You think this is bad," he'd say. "Someday, I'm going to get you alone. Then you'll find out what bad really is."

Just before Christmas break a message came to me during math class. I was to report to the office immediately. I was afraid something had happened to my dad; I was always afraid of that. He's not like drunk fathers in books. They're always no-good bastards who even beat their kids and their wives. My dad never hit me; never yelled at me. He was just a drunk.

I hustled down the main hallway, turned into a side hall that led to the office, and came face to face with Miller and one of his friends. Miller grabbed me, spun me around, and put his hand over my mouth. Then the two of them dragged me into the boys' bathroom and kicked open the door to one of the stalls. They flipped me over and started dunking my head into a toilet that was full of crap and piss. I wanted to scream, but I had to hold my breath. They'd pull me up; I'd gulp some air; and then they'd dunk me again. After doing that six or seven times, they started flushing the toilet. I'd hear the roar of the water and the two of them laughing, then more roaring and more laughter. Finally, after what seemed like an hour but was probably a minute, they dropped me. My head smacked against the porcelain toilet bowl.

I ended up on my knees, gasping for breath, with snot coming out of my nose and toilet water dripping out of my hair. Miller leaned down close to me. "Your old man got kicked out of the army for being a piece-of-crap coward, and you're just like him." With that, he and his friend were gone.

A couple of minutes later some big guy, one of the football players wearing his letterman's jacket, came into the bathroom. I was sitting on the floor, crying and shaking. My face was bruised and my nose was bleeding. He picked me up by the shoulders, led me over to the sink, turned the faucet on, and then stood by me as I splashed warm water onto my face.

He stayed with me until I'd cleaned myself up and the shaking and crying had stopped. "I got to get back to class," he said at last. "But you tell Ms. Dugan who did this to you, and she'll take care of them."

"I will," I said, my voice shaky.

But I never did.

CHAPTER THREE

Now that same Brent Miller was back at Lincoln High, playing war hero. He stood at attention, looking out over the class. When our eyes caught, there was a quick flash of recognition. He smirked at me, and it was as if no time at all had passed, as if he were still holding me over the toilet. I quickly looked away. I wanted to keep my eyes turned away; I wanted to stare at those greedy birds and that green grass, but I just couldn't keep myself from looking back.

And I couldn't keep from listening either. Miller's voice was cool and confident. Someday he was going to be a tank commander. He hoped he'd be assigned to Iraq. He'd only been in the service nine months, but already he'd learned about teamwork and dedication and patriotism. Being in the army was the greatest job in the world.

Everybody else was falling for his patriotic trash, but I knew him for what he was—a loser who'd joined the army because he had no place else to go other than jail. As he droned on, waves of heat rolled over me, followed by waves of cold. The whole time my stomach churned. I wanted the hour to end, but time crawled along. What made it worse was that Heather Carp and Melody Turner and their whole group gaped at Miller as if he really were a war hero.

Finally he stopped. I thought it was over, that he'd leave, but Arnold came to his side. "Private Miller would be willing to answer a few questions, if you have any."

Brian Mitchell, who was in some sort of marine training already, shot his hand up. "Are you afraid of dying?"

Miller cleared his throat. "If I have to die for my country, I will. And if I have to kill for my country, I'll do that too." It was as if he were a really bad actor in some really bad war movie.

"Any other questions?" Mr. Arnold asked, looking around. No hands waved about. I let out a sigh of relief. But just as Miller was about to leave, Melody Turner raised her hand.

As usual, Melody was stuffed into a tank top two sizes too small for her, and she twisted sideways in her seat so he'd be sure to notice. She gave him her bad-girl smile and bit the end of her pencil. "This is a little off the topic," she said, "but what do army privates do for fun?"

Heather Carp and her other friends giggled; Miller grinned. "The same things you like to do, I'd bet," he said.

"Maybe we should get together, then," Melody said.

The class roared. Arnold waved his hands around like a cop trying to keep a car from driving into a ditch. "All right," he said, smiling, "that's enough of that."

Melody picked at her fingernails. "You said you wanted questions."

"I know I did, Melody," Arnold said. "But I meant serious questions." He looked out. "Does anyone have one?"

That's when Melissa Watts raised her hand.

CHAPTER FOUR

should have known she would. Her binder is plastered with stickers that read WAR IS TERRORISM and WAR SUCKS. When she was a junior, she wrote an article for the school newspaper about the rights of gay students. Most kids don't like her much, but I've always thought she was OK.

I've known her for a long time. She runs cross-country, which is the sport I used to do before the divorce, back when I did sports. For a while I was the only person at Whittier School who could beat her. Our races always played out the same way. Even then she was tall and slender, and she'd eat up ground with her long stride, but I'd catch and pass her at the very end. She has green eyes, and as I raced by her to the finish line, those eyes would spit fire at me. I like that about her, too.

Arnold nodded to her. "What's your question, Melissa?"

"I was just wondering," she said, "if Private Miller has ever read about the places he might end up. You know what I mean. Stuff on the history of the Middle East, or on Islam?"

It was a trap. Everybody in the classroom knew it except Miller. Melissa had the jaws ready to snap shut, and Miller walked right in. "Sure," he said. "I've read stuff about the Middle East."

Melissa made a big point of taking out her pen and opening up her notebook. "That's great. Could you give me titles of books you'd recommend?"

Miller's face reddened. "Titles? I'm not sure I can remember any titles."

Melissa leaned forward. "How about authors, then? Just one or two to get me started. You must remember some names."

Heather Carp turned in her seat and glared at Melissa. "You are such a bitch."

"Heather," Arnold said angrily.

"Well, it's true, Mr. Arnold. You know what she's doing."

Melissa's voice hardened. "If he hasn't read anything, why doesn't he just say so?" She looked at Miller. "You haven't read anything on the Middle East, have you? You're just saying exactly what the army tells you to say."

"Stop it, Melissa," Arnold said.

"Why do I have to stop it? We're all pretending he's some sort of expert just because he has a uniform on, but he doesn't know anything."

"I said stop it," Arnold repeated sharply. "Right now."

The whole class had turned on Melissa. They were all glaring at her. I couldn't leave her hanging out there alone. Not with Miller.

"What are you getting mad at her for?" I said, and now the class wheeled around to look at me. "She asked a simple question. Either he's read some books or he hasn't." I forced myself to look right at Miller. "So what's your answer? Yes or no?"

Miller stared back at me for a while, and then he looked down. "I haven't had time to read anything yet, but I will."

There was an awkward silence, and then Arnold started talking, going through all the regular thank you and good luck stuff. The class clapped; Miller mumbled something; the class clapped again. Finally, Miller left.

With Miller gone, Arnold passed out an article on the Israelis and the Palestinians. The pages were all wrinkled and dirty; my copy had to have been at least ten years old. "Read this for tomorrow. Read it slowly and think about it as you go. And don't lose it; I want it back."

I put my head down and started reading the words, but it was too complicated for me to follow. When the bell rang, I took my time packing my stuff into my backpack. By the time I started for the door, all the other kids were gone. As I passed by Arnold's desk, he raised his head from the papers in front of him. He looked like he was about to say something, but then his eyes returned to his desk.

I was out.

CHAPTER FIVE

When I reached my locker, I shoved my books inside, slammed the door shut, and then started down the hallway toward the main doors. I hadn't taken more than three steps when I heard Melissa's voice. "Chance, wait up a second. OK?"

Her locker was across the hall and down from mine. I turned back and watched as she pulled a red jacket out of her locker and tied it around her waist. She closed her locker and walked quickly to where I stood. "My hands are shaking so much I couldn't get my locker open," she said.

She fell into stride with me as I headed for the exit, and she started talking to me as if we walked together out of the building every day. "Arnold makes me so mad," she said. "He's always lecturing us about the wonders of the Constitution and the Bill of Rights, but he only believes in free speech in a book. Practice free speech in real life, get somebody mad at you because of what you say, and all of a sudden he's got his hand over your mouth, trying to muzzle you."

We'd reached the main door. I opened it, let Melissa go first, and then stepped outside. Once I felt the fresh air on my face, I realized I'd been burning alive in that building. "I'll see you around, Melissa," I said, and started down the stairs. She reached out and took hold of my forearm.

"Wait, Chance," she said. "Come with me to Java John's. I really feel like talking to somebody."

"I don't know, Melissa. I've got to—"

"Please, Chance. Just for a few minutes."

I didn't know what to say. It had been a long time since anyone had asked me to do anything. I shrugged. "OK. But just for a couple minutes."

Java John's is opposite the west side of campus. When we turned the corner by the A building, we saw Melody and Heather and a couple of their friends. They had formed a semicircle around Brent Miller, as if he were some sort of rock star and they were his adoring groupies.

Melissa and I instinctively started walking faster, hoping to get by unseen. We almost made it too. But Heather's voice reached out and caught us. "Bitch," she taunted. I would have kept going, but Melissa turned back.

"Shut up, Heather."

"Shut up yourself," Heather snapped back.

Miller stepped toward me. "You had a lot to say in that classroom, Chance. How come you're so quiet now?"

He took another step toward me, and then another. His

hands curled into fists. When he was a yard away, he stopped. "Here I am. Take your best shot."

I had no chance. Miller was bigger, older, stronger—and he'd had training. Heather and Melody and the other girls were looking at me, their eyes gleaming with excitement. They wanted to see a fight; they wanted to see me get my face pounded in. Melissa grabbed my arm and pulled on it. "Let it go, Chance," she said. "Let's just get out of here."

I wanted to hit Miller. For a moment, I wanted to hit him more than I wanted anything in the world. But I was afraid of him too. So I let Melissa pull me away.

"You're a coward," he called after me. "Always were and always will be. Just like your old man."

CHAPTER SIX

"Let's just skip this," I said once we'd crossed the street and were standing in front of Java John's.

Melissa shook her head. "I'm not going to let those morons ruin my day." She pulled the door open, and there wasn't much else for me to do but follow her in.

At the counter stood a dark-haired guy with a little goatee. Melissa looked at the menu board and ordered a latte and an almond biscotti. "You can pick it up at the end of the counter," the guy said after she paid. "What can I get you?" he asked as I stepped up to the cash register.

I felt in my pocket for change. I had three quarters and some dimes and nickels—enough for a coffee but nothing more.

"Size?"

"Small."

"Anything to eat?"

I shook my head. He pushed a button on the register. "That'll be a dollar eight."

I'd forgotten about tax. I pulled the change out of my pocket and laid it on the counter. I was three cents short. He reached to a little plate with pennies on it, took three, and added it to my coins.

Melissa was sitting at the only window table. I carried my coffee there and sat down. "Don't let him get to you," she said. "You're not the coward. He's the coward."

I took a sip of the coffee. It was bitter, and I wanted to get away from her. "I need to get some sugar," I said, and I went back up to the counter.

When I returned, she fiddled with her cup a little, and then looked at me again. "You were brave in class today, Chance. You were the only one who was. Fighting isn't the only way to be brave, you know."

"Could we talk about something else?"

For a long time we both sat, neither of us saying anything. Then she smiled. "Let's talk about the *Lincoln Light.*"

I wasn't sure I'd heard right. "You mean the school newspaper?"

"Yeah. I'm the editor, you know."

I shook my head. "No, I didn't know."

"Well, I am. And I'm looking for writers. People who are willing to take on controversial topics. I think you'd be great."

So that was it—that's why she'd wanted to talk to me. "I can't write for the *Lincoln Light,* Melissa."

"Why not?"

"I've got nothing to say."

"Everybody has something to say. You write about things you care about."

"I don't care about anything."

"Yes, you do," she said, her voice angry. "Otherwise you wouldn't have said what you said in class today. You care about the truth." She paused. "At least think about it, OK? We meet every other Friday night at the Blue Note Café. It's up on Thirty-second Avenue, at the top of the stairwell that leads down to the beach. Even if you didn't write, you could help with proofreading and stuff like that. We need new people, Chance. Besides, what else are you doing?"

I looked into her eyes. They were open and honest. She wasn't pretending—she really did want me to join her newspaper staff.

"I'll think about it," I said.

"OK," she said. She took a sip of her latte, finished her biscotti, and then stood. "I've got to get going. See you tomorrow."

CHAPTER SEVEN

I sat at the table and finished my coffee. With a couple of packets of sugar added to it, it was OK. Besides, I'd paid for it, so I was going to drink it. When the cup was empty, I stayed where I was, looking out the window. The door opened and a couple of older women came in. They placed their orders and then glanced over at me. They wanted the window table. I stood up, pushed in the chair, tossed my cup into the trash, and headed for the door. "Come again," the guy behind the counter called out as I left.

Usually I walk down to the sailboat along Sixty-fifth Street, but that day I went three blocks south to Sixty-second. Just past the community center is the little house where I used to live.

It had been a long time since I'd walked by that house. All over Seattle, new owners have rebuilt older homes, making them so big it's hard to recognize the original house. But other than the bushes being a little taller and a fresh coat of yellow paint, my old house looked the same as it had on the day I'd left it.

I stopped across the street from it and raised my eyes to the second story. Behind a tall, thin window was my bedroom—or what had been my bedroom. It was small, with steeply pitched walls. I had a dartboard on the door and a *Star Wars* poster tacked to the wall. Hidden beneath that poster was a hole in the wallboard about the size of an orange. My dad always said he was going to fix it, but he never did. I wondered if the new owners had done anything about it. For some reason, I hoped they hadn't.

It didn't seem as if anyone was home, so I crossed the street, walked down the driveway, and peered over the chain-link fence into the back yard. The yard looked the same, too, though it was smaller than I'd remembered. The laurel bushes where I'd built my forts were still there. So were the plum tree and the patch of grass where on hot days I'd run through the sprinkler.

It was on that patch of grass that my mom had told me. I didn't understand what she was saying at first. "I'm dying here," she said, and I thought she was sick with cancer or something like that. I guess my fear showed in my face, because she pulled me close to her then, held my head against her chest. "Not my body, Chance. My heart. My soul. I'm dying. I've got to start my life over. Away from your father. You understand why, don't you?"

I shook my head no, but I did understand. I'd heard them arguing at night. I knew my dad drank way too much and worked way too little. "You won't leave me too, will you?" I said.

"No, Chance. I won't ever leave you. I promise."

I was still staring into the yard when the front door of the house opened and a little red-haired girl about nine years old stepped out, her mother right behind her. The little girl's eyes caught mine, and she immediately smiled, but her mother didn't.

"I used to live here," I said quickly. "I was just curious about the house and the yard."

The woman reached out and grabbed her daughter's hand. I backed away from the yard, then turned and walked quickly down the street. I didn't have to turn back to know the woman's eyes were on me.

CHAPTER EIGHT

A few minutes later I was heading down the steep ramp that leads from the Shilshole Bay Marina parking lot to Pier B, where my dad's sailboat is moored. At the bottom of the ramp is a locked gate that keeps the snoops and the thieves out. I stuck my key in the lock, turned the handle, and stepped onto the pier, making sure the gate closed and locked behind me. Then I walked past a couple dozen sailboats until I reached the *Tiny Dancer*.

I was home.

When kids hear I live on a boat, they picture a floating mansion outlined with strings of white Christmas lights like the one in the old movie *Sleepless in Seattle*. They think I sit on the deck under an umbrella while waves gently lap up against the sides, foghorns sound in the distance, and exotic seabirds fly overhead. But I don't live on any floating mansion; the *Tiny Dancer* is an old, weather-beaten thirty-foot sailboat. The paint is blistered and peeling. Barnacles and seaweed cling fore and aft. Before she could sail anywhere, she'd need to be hauled out and completely gone over, but that costs money and lots of it.

Which is another way of saying that even though I live on a sailboat, I'm not a sailor. Mainmast, capstan, jib, boom, tiller, rudder, port, starboard, bow, stern—I know what most of that nautical crap means. But nobody learns how to tack into the wind by sitting on a sailboat, and sitting is all I've ever done. My dad hasn't taken the boat out into Puget Sound for five years. I know as much about sailing as some guy living in a mobile home knows about driving in the Indianapolis 500.

Mr. Kovich and Mr. Nelson and other guys with boats on our pier tell me the *Tiny Dancer* is a decent sailboat, so I guess it is, but it's a lousy place to live. It's so small that my dad and I can hardly turn around without bumping into each other. All our belongings have to fit into the little nooks and crannies in the cramped cabin below deck. The galley has a tiny oven, a tiny sink, and a couple of tiny shelves for food. The refrigerator isn't really a refrigerator—it's an icebox about the size of an old stereo speaker. The table in the galley barely holds two plates and two glasses. In the main part of the cabin are two side benches. Above them are small storage areas and then a pair of narrow, rectangular windows. I sleep up front in the V berth; my dad sleeps aft. When I first slept on the boat, I sat up quickly in the mornings a couple of times, cracking my head pretty good. Since then, I've always remembered to crawl in and crawl out.

We're moored at slip 45, which puts us about halfway down the pier. When I came even with slip 31, I saw my dad sitting on deck. He was smoking a cigarette and staring at the million-dollar yachts a couple of piers away.

He shouldn't have been there.

All summer, he'd worked from noon to nine at the Sunset West Condominiums, a two-hundred-unit waterfront retirement apartment complex just down the road from the marina. He unclogged toilets, washed windows, cleaned the laundry room, vacuumed the halls, moved sofas—whatever the old people wanted done, he did. It was a crappy job, but it was a job, the first steady job he'd had for as long as I can remember. It kept him from drinking at all during the day, and maybe kept him from drinking as much as he used to at night, though I'm not sure about that.

"What's going on, Dad?" I said as I stepped up onto the boat.

"Nothing's going on," he said, not even looking at me.

I settled onto the bench across from him. "Shouldn't you be at work?"

He leaned down and picked up a brown paper bag by his feet. I didn't have to look to know that inside was a pint of vodka. He took a sip, and then looked out across the water again.

"Why aren't you at work?"

He turned to face me. "Because I got fired."

"What happened?

He stubbed out his cigarette, stuffed his bottle of vodka into the pocket of his jacket, and stood. "I'm going down to Little Coney. Get some coffee and see if Frank Fisher's there. I'll be back late."

Once he was gone, I sat on the bench and looked at nothing. We were in trouble. Again.

My dad owned the sailboat outright. He bought it with the money he'd gotten from selling the house after the divorce. But there was still the monthly moorage fee and the sewage fee and the electricity bill and the heat bill and food and soap and toilet paper and toothpaste and a hundred other things. He'd want his cigarettes and his booze. Where was the money going to come from? He'd used up all his welfare eligibility. I made some money washing pots on weekends at Ray's restaurant, but I already gave my dad most of what I earned to pay for food. The money I kept I used to buy my clothes and my shoes and stuff I needed for school like notebooks and paper. But even if I gave him every single penny I earned, it wouldn't be enough to pay all the bills. It wouldn't even be close.

I looked out at the water. Four ducks were swimming in the oily gunk between Pier B and Pier C. All they had to do was spread their wings and fly away, but they stayed. How stupid can you get?

CHAPTER NINE

The joke is that according to the divorce papers, I'm supposed to be living with my mom. For a while, I did. After the divorce, she landed a job at Dakota Art Store in the Roosevelt district. We lived in an apartment right above the store. Sometimes at night we'd go back down into the store after dinner. I'd sit and watch as she'd stand before a big easel and paint using stuff customers had returned. "This is crap," she told me, even though all her paintings looked great to me. "When I get enough money, I'm going to art school. Then you'll see what I can do. The whole world will see what I can do."

I stayed with her during the week, and then went to stay with my dad on the sailboat Saturday, Saturday night, and Sunday. He was drinking, and after the first time the boat was no fun. I couldn't wait for Sunday night when my mom would pick me up.

Only one Sunday she didn't show. Dad called her from the phone booth outside the marina office, but her phone just rang and rang. We took the bus to the apartment and knocked on the door. No answer. Dad tried the doorknob. It opened, and we stepped inside.

The apartment was bare except for three boxes by the front door. Dad opened them one at a time. Inside were my clothes, a football, an old school binder, some baseball cards, and a couple of books. From behind us came a voice. "Are you looking for Marlene?"

We turned around. Standing outside the door was Bill, the man who lived in the apartment across the hall from Mom and me.

"Yeah," Dad said. "We are."

"She moved out yesterday." Bill looked at me. "I thought that you . . ." He stopped.

"Did she say where she was going?" Dad asked.

"Some town along the Oregon coast. Not Cannon Beach, but somewhere near there." He stopped. "I'm sorry. I didn't pay attention to the name."

My dad didn't say anything to me on the bus ride back to the marina, but when we got to the sailboat he ruffled my hair. "It'll be OK, Chance. She'll call. You'll see her real soon."

Mom's letter arrived a couple weeks later. Dad read it, and then handed it to me. I didn't understand most of it, but there was one sentence that I read over and over: *It will only be for a little while.*

Those days Dad was full of plans. At night, after we ate, he drank his vodka and read me passages from *Sailing Alone around the World,* his favorite book. "We'll be like Joshua

Slocum. We'll sail someplace special. No school for you; no crummy jobs for me. How's that sound?"

"Sounds great," I said, but all the time I kept waiting for Mom to come back and get me. The weeks turned into months, and all I did was slop around in the marina, watch my dad drink, and listen to his stories about the sailing trips we were going to take.

One night, when Mom had been gone for five months, he pulled out his nautical charts for what had to be the fiftieth time. "I was talking to Frank Fisher today," he said, his words slurred. "The way Frank figures it, the way to sail around the world is to do it in stages. First we'd go to Hawaii. I'd get a job there for a while, and then—"

"We're never going anywhere," I said, interrupting him.

"Sure, we are," he said.

"No, we're not," I said, my voice rising with every word, all the anger spilling out. "And Mom's never coming back either. You're a drunk and that's all you are. So just shut up! OK? Just shut up and leave me alone!"

He looked at me for a long time. Then he folded up his charts and put them away.

That was years ago. He has never mentioned sailing around the world to me since that day. But every once in a while he'll put out his charts and pore over them as if he really is going somewhere someday. And sometimes, when I get the mail from the woman at the marina office, there will be a letter with handwriting that reminds me of my mom's. My whole body will go tense, and then I'll see that it's from Green-lake Golf or Funtasia, and I'll feel like a fool.

CHAPTER TEN

I sat on the deck of the *Tiny Dancer* watching the stupid ducks for about fifteen minutes, and then I did what I always do when I feel like my head is about to explode: I ran.

Running is the only thing I've ever really liked to do. Sometimes at Lincoln I look at the kids on the track team or the cross-country team on the day of a meet. They've got their hundred-dollar running shoes, their fifty-dollar running shorts, their bottles of Gatorade, and their energy bars. But I'd beaten all of them in elementary school, and I still figured I could beat them. They had a softness to them, in their eyes, a softness that made me believe I could gut it out at the end against them, and take them, if I ever got the chance. "Finish strong," my dad always told me. "Finish strong."

That day I ran my normal route. I started by heading east on Seaview Avenue toward the Ballard Locks. For the first mile or so, my mind was buzzing like a chainsaw. I had conversations with Melissa Watts and Brent Miller and Mr. Arnold and my dad. But by the time I'd reached the locks, my mind shut off just like it always does. Instead of thinking while I ran, I was just running. Through the locks, up the hill, and over the footbridge to Magnolia—one foot after the other.

At the end of the footbridge, I stopped for a minute and looked out. A Coast Guard cutter was going through the locks, headed from Lake Union toward Puget Sound. Some herons were flying from their nests above the railroad tracks out toward the water.

I watched for a couple of minutes and then I ran back the same way I'd come: through the locks, then along Seaview Avenue to Pier B. I kept going, past the marina offices and out to Golden Gardens Park. At Meadow Point, I cut over to the beach and ran in the sand toward North Beach.

At the spot where the beach turns north is a weather-beaten maple tree that seems to grow sideways right out of the rocks. My mom always said it had to be the toughest tree in the world. I don't know how it gets the nutrients to stay alive, or why it doesn't blow over in the windstorms that come every winter, but somehow it survives. I kept going until I reached that maple, touched it for luck, and then headed back.

When I reached Pier B, I looked at my watch. I'd run seven miles in a little over forty minutes. I went onto the boat, grabbed some clean clothes and a towel from the cabin, and headed back up the ramp.

In the parking lot across from Pier B is an L-shaped utility room with lockers, a washer and a dryer, toilets, and some shower stalls. It's open only to people who have a boat in the marina. I stuck my key into the lock, turned the handle, and stepped inside.

As usual, it was empty. I walked past the lockers and the washing machines, turned right, and entered the shower area. There are three stalls; I took the one farthest back. For the next twenty minutes, I let the water wash away the sweat and dirt of the day. After twenty minutes, the water slowly changed from hot to warm. Before it turned cold, I stepped out, toweled myself dry, and put on clean clothes. Then I went back to the boat.

I had six hours to kill before I could flick off the lights and call it a day. I waited until it was almost seven before I heated up a can of tomato soup and made a grilled cheese sandwich. After I'd cleaned the dishes and put them away, I watched *Fear Factor* and *Cops* on TV. When that got too stupid, I switched off the television and turned on the radio. There are kids at school who live for music; I wish I were that way. I wish I could find some station that would make an hour or two or three go by, but I can't.

Around nine o'clock I left the boat and walked the length of the marina. I like to walk after it gets dark because it's quiet then. The sidewalks are empty and the nightclubs haven't gotten going.

It was after eleven when I finally climbed into my berth, and my dad was still out drinking. The wind was up, making the boat rock back and forth, and my mind would rock back and forth with it. One minute I'd want him to disappear from my life forever; the next I'd panic at the thought of being alone in the world.

I don't know when I finally fell asleep. When the alarm went off at six-thirty, my dad was snoring away in his berth. I didn't know whether I was glad to see him there, or whether I wished he hadn't come back.

I closed my eyes and lay back. I thought about skipping school, but if I did I'd end up hanging around the boat waiting for him to start drinking. So at seven-fifteen I was dragging myself up Sixty-first toward Lincoln High.

CHAPTER ELEVEN

Sixty-first crosses under the railroad tracks before it climbs the bluff into Ballard. Homeless guys sleep behind the blackberry bushes that grow along the tracks. Most of the time I just hear them rustling around back there, but sometimes they come out and ask for money or cigarettes.

The guy who came out that morning had a skinny, wrinkled face, blue eyes, and long, black hair. "You got a spare quarter, kid?" he said, his voice raspy.

"I got nothing," I said.

I tried to edge around him, but he stepped in front of me.

"Have a heart, kid," he said. "A quarter? A dime? You got to have something."

"I told you," I snapped. "I got nothing."

As I moved by him, he grabbed at my sleeve. I wheeled around and pushed him away. His chest felt small and bony, like a child's. He toppled in a heap onto the sidewalk.

"All I wanted was a quarter," he called after me. "You didn't have to hit me, you son of a bitch."

It wasn't until I'd reached the top of the hill that I looked back. The guy was sitting on the sidewalk, looking up at me. "You son of a bitch," he called out again, but his voice was so weak I could hardly hear him. I kept going.

It's straight uphill from the marina to Thirty-second Avenue, but there the land levels. Walter's Café is on Thirty-second, right at the top of the hill. Kim Lawton—a friend of my mom's from before the divorce—works there. She's always after me to stop in to see her, but I don't, partly because I don't have much money and partly because she reminds me of my mother. But the whole thing with the homeless bum made my hands shaky and my knees feel like they were made of water. A cup of something hot didn't seem like the worst idea.

Kim was behind the counter. The instant she saw me, her face broke into a big grin. "Good to see you, stranger," she said as I stepped inside. "And it's about time, too."

I ordered a small hot chocolate and put six quarters down on the counter. She pushed the coins back to me. "Go sit down," she said. "I'll bring it to you."

I found an empty table in the corner. I hadn't waited for more than a minute before Kim put a mug of hot chocolate on the table and settled into the chair across from me. "How are things going, Chance?" she said.

"OK."

"What's OK mean?"

"OK means OK. Not good, not bad."

She pursed her lips, and I could tell we were both thinking

about my mom. Just then an old guy came in. Kim jumped up and returned to her spot behind the counter. "The regular?" she asked.

The old guy nodded, and soon the café filled with the sound of the espresso machine. My chocolate was too hot to drink quickly, so I put my hands around the mug and let the warmth in, taking a sip every now and then.

I thought that sitting would steady my nerves; instead, it made things worse. I kept seeing the homeless guy sprawled out on the sidewalk. I kept feeling his bony chest against my palms. He was the size of a child and I'd pushed him hard. What if I'd hurt him badly? What if he was still down on the sidewalk?

More customers came in. Kim looked over at me, shrugged, and I gave her a wave to show I understood. Eventually I finished my hot chocolate and then headed for the door. "You leaving?" Kim called to me. She had a line of customers now.

"I've got school," I said.

"Come in Saturday when it's not so busy," she said. "I want to have a long talk with you."

"I will," I said.

I pushed the door open, but instead of going to school, I retraced my steps to the top of the hill and looked down the street to where the homeless guy had fallen. He wasn't there. I wanted to believe that meant everything was OK, but I couldn't. He might have crawled into the bushes. If he did, and he was hurt and alone, he could die in there and nobody would find him for weeks.

I walked slowly down to the bottom of the hill. When I

reached the spot where he'd fallen, I stepped off the sidewalk and pushed my way through the tangle of blackberry bushes. "Anybody in here?" I called out.

There was no answer.

"Is somebody in here?"

Still no answer.

I followed a hint of a trail about twenty more feet, ducked under some vines, and found myself in a small clearing. Under a makeshift tent made of plastic bags were some cans of food, a pair of boots, an old coat, a sleeping bag, empty beer bottles, and a bunch of old magazines. Sitting on the ground next to that pile of junk were two guys—the guy I'd pushed and another guy who was older, skinnier, and had a long, gray beard. They were both smoking cigarettes.

"You OK?" I said, looking at the guy I'd pushed. He just stared at me. "You OK?" I repeated. He kept staring.

I reached into my pocket, pulled out the quarters that Kim Lawton hadn't taken, and held them out to him. He stuck his hand out. There was an open sore on his palm, and his hand was filthy. I placed the coins into his hand and he shut his fingers tightly around them.

"I'm sorry," I said. "I didn't mean to hurt you." Then I turned and got of there as fast as I could.

CHAPTER TWELVE

By the time I reached Lincoln High that morning, I'd missed all of first and half of second period. Mrs. Spielman, the attendance secretary, chewed me out. "You can't get credits if you cut classes," she said as she wrote out my pass.

"I haven't cut many classes," I said. "Besides, school has only been going a couple of weeks."

"Well begun is half done, and don't forget it."

All morning I sat in the back of whatever class I was in and tuned out everything. During lunch I went to the commons area, bought a Coke out of the machine, sat in a corner, and drank it.

I tried to tune out everything there too, but three girls came and sat at the same table. They'd talk a little, and then start laughing so hard their heads bobbed up and down. Then they'd talk some more, and then they'd laugh again. Just before the lunch period ended, I spotted Melissa Watts. She was talking to Rachel Miller, another girl in Arnold's class. I kept hoping she'd look over and see me, but she didn't, and then the lunch period ended.

I thought about cutting my afternoon classes. The *Tiny Dancer* would probably be empty. My dad might be looking for a job, although it was more likely he was out looking for a drink. But what would I do when I got to the boat? Cutting school would just make the day longer.

So when sixth period rolled around, I was sitting in my normal place in the last chair in the last row in Mr. Arnold's class. The starlings were still attacking the bugs in the lawn, and Arnold still wanted to talk about terrorism and Iraq and all that crap.

I've got to give it to Arnold. The guy worked hard to make class interesting. But without Brent Miller in uniform right in the front of the class, kids didn't pay attention. Heather Carp was picking nail polish off her fingernails; Melody Turner was doodling in her notebook.

Class ended with Arnold and Melissa arguing about countries I couldn't have found on a map and leaders whose names I couldn't begin to spell. A couple of times Melissa would look back at me, but I couldn't make myself care about Singapore or Indonesia. All I could think about was the moorage fee, the electric bill, the heating bill, the sewage fee, the food bills— and how we didn't have money to pay any of them.

When I reached my locker, Melissa was waiting for me. "Why didn't you say anything? You just sat there all through class."

Her eyes were both angry and disappointed. How could I explain? She lived in a big house overlooking Puget Sound. She drove a brand-new blue Jetta, wore hundred-dollar shoes and hundred-dollar pants and hundred-dollar shirts.

I closed my locker. "I've got to go," I said. "I'll see you tomorrow." Before she could say anything else, I walked away.

CHAPTER THIRTEEN

Ever since I turned fifteen I've worked weekends washing pots at Ray's restaurant, a fancy fish place right down from Pier B, from two to ten. It's hot, sweaty work. The water is almost boiling, the garbage cans stink of fish guts, and I have to hunch over the whole time. The only good thing about the job is the money, and there isn't much of that.

My boss is Jeff Creager, a big guy with a big voice who is always worked up about something. Everybody stays clear of him if they can. When I stepped into the kitchen the Saturday after my dad got fired, Creager was by the grill, arguing with the chef, Carl Thorgenson. Instead of going to the sink, I went over to Creager. "I've got to talk to you," I said.

"Not now," he snapped, and he started going on about some salmon recipe Thorgenson wanted to use. I stood listening to them yell at each other about how much pepper was too much, wondering if they'd ever stop. The other kitchen-help guys were peeling potatoes or chopping lettuce, all the time sneaking peeks over at me, wondering what I was doing. Finally Creager stopped for a moment and glared at me. "Didn't I tell you to get to work?"

"I've got to talk to you," I said.

"This better be important," he said.

My throat went dry. I licked my lips and then swallowed. "I need more hours," I said.

He laughed sarcastically, and then motioned to the entire work crew. "You hear him? He says he needs more hours. Well, I'll tell you and I'll tell everyone. I've got no more hours to give."

"You don't understand, Mr. Creager," I said. "I've—"

"I do understand," he said, interrupting. "Your old man lost that job over at Sunset West. I heard about it. It's a tough break for you. But this isn't a church, Chance. This is a business, and right now business isn't good. You're lucky to have the hours you've got. So put on your apron and get busy."

I did what he said, and for the rest of that afternoon I stopped thinking about anything but the greasy pots and the hot water and the steam—and how much I hated them all. When my shift ended, I was too tired to worry about money or my father or anything. I just went back to the boat and slept.

You can't think about something all the time, no matter how important it is. For the next few weeks my mind would go back and forth between long periods of a vague drifting and short times of intense focus. When my mind was drifting, my dad's drinking, the moorage fees, school—none of it seemed to matter much. The blood in my body and the thoughts in my brain moved slowly like a wide river close to the ocean. But every once in a while I'd snap out of that state and everything would seem as sharp as if it were under a microscope. Sometimes all I could think about was money. I'd look around and it seemed like every kid but me had it. Money for cars, money for clothes, money for movies, money for CD players, money for cell phones. Walking home after school I'd watch the Lexuses and the Mercedes pull out of the parking lot, the owners hidden behind tinted glass. I'd look at the houses on Sunset Hill with their fancy landscaping and their statues and fountains. All of it cost money, lots of money, money that all these people had. How could money be so easy to get for some people and so hard for others?

When the end of the month finally came, I told myself that I wasn't going to ask my dad about the moorage fee. There was no point, because I knew the answer. But when I got back to the boat in the afternoon and saw him sitting topside smoking a cigarette and reading the newspaper like some retired rich guy, I couldn't stop myself. "Did you pay the moorage fee?" I said as soon as I stepped onto the boat.

He looked up from the newspaper. "What?"

"The moorage fee," I repeated. "It's due today. Did you pay it?"

"Don't worry about the moorage fee, Chance. They can't touch us for three months. It's the law. By then I'll have a job."

"What if you don't get a job?"

"I will get a job."

"Can you get unemployment compensation?"

"No. I can't get it. My job wasn't that kind of job. And I can't get welfare anymore either."

"So what are we going to do?"

"I told you. I'm going to get a job."

He held the newspaper up in front of him so that I couldn't see his face. I went down below, shoved my backpack under the navigation table, and made myself a cheese sandwich. As I was eating, he leaned down into the companionway. "I'm going out," he said. "I'll be back later."

When I finished the sandwich, I sat at the table thinking. Three months. It wasn't long. What would we do then? Sell the boat? Who'd buy it? There had to be twenty boats for sale in the marina in better shape than the *Tiny Dancer*. Besides, without the boat, where would we live?

I ran that day, but instead of going through the locks and up into Magnolia, I kept going on Market until I reached Little City Hall. I pushed around some brochures on a table, hoping to spot what I was looking for. Behind the counter was a guy with long hair and a beard. "Can I help you find something?" he said.

"There's this family I know that doesn't have much money. I was thinking they might be eligible for food stamps. Is there some sort of application form?"

"It's right there," he said. "Right where you're looking. In green."

I picked up the form. "Thanks," I said, folding it and putting it in my back pocket. "I'll bring this to them."

I ran back to the marina, the whole time feeling stupid for

lying. The guy had seen right through me. After I showered, I went back to the boat, sat down at the navigation table, and filled out the food stamp application. Then I addressed an envelope, stuck a stamp on it, and put it on the table where my dad would see it. The only thing left for him to do was write down his social security number, sign it, and drop it in the mail. But even as I left it there, I knew he never would.

CHAPTER FOURTEEN

That Saturday I slept in for as long as I could, ate a little breakfast, and killed the rest of the morning watching television. In the afternoon I headed for my job at Ray's.

Eight hours later, tired and sweaty, I made my way back to the empty boat. They gave me a free dinner at work, but I was hungry again, so I heated up a frozen pizza, turned on the television, and watched an old movie about gamblers that was supposed to be funny but wasn't.

The movie ended at twelve-thirty. I flicked off the television, crawled into my berth, and fell asleep. I woke up around three in the morning. Immediately I recognized the sound that had awakened me: my dad was walking back and forth on the deck.

I looked out the small, rectangular window. It was raining, and the wind was blowing. I lay on my back for a minute hoping he'd come down. Finally I threw the blankets back, pulled my coat on, and climbed to the top stair. "What are you doing, Dad?" I said, leaning my head out. "You're going to get sick."

He stopped pacing and looked at me. "Wouldn't it be something to be out sailing tonight, Chance? Wouldn't it?"

"You're going to get sick," I repeated. "Come down below."

He looked up at the sky and then he looked at me. "I'm going to get a job, Chance. You don't believe me, and I don't blame you, but I will. And I'm going to sail this boat someday too. You wait and see if I don't."

He'd been drunk that night, but on Sunday afternoon he got a haircut and on Sunday night he did a couple of loads of wash. All that week he was up before me. By the time I crawled out of my berth, he'd already shaved, combed his hair, and put on his best shirt and pants. When I came back from running in the afternoon, he'd be at the table in the cabin circling ads in the help-wanted section of the *Seattle Times*.

Wednesday night the fat guy from the marina office came down onto the pier. "You've got a phone call," he called to my dad. "Salmon Bay Gravel."

My dad hustled up the pier to the office. When he came back, he didn't say anything, so I asked. "What was that about?"

"I've got an interview tomorrow. Cement work."

About a hundred questions popped into my head, but I knew to keep my mouth shut. He wouldn't want to talk until he actually had the job, and I didn't blame him.

Thursday morning he shaved, and then shaved again. He took my math book and used it to smooth out some of the creases on his gray shirt. "You look fine, Dad," I told him. "You really do."

All day at school I kept thinking of him at that interview. I couldn't figure how it could go wrong. He hadn't had a drink all week. And when he wasn't drinking, my dad was an OK guy and a good, hard worker. Besides, it wasn't like he was applying to be a brain surgeon.

When school ended, I hurried back to the marina. As soon as I stepped onto the boat, I called out for him. "You here, Dad?" I said, climbing down into the cabin. On the table sat an empty bottle of beer. In the trash were a half dozen more.

It made me angry. OK, my dad drank. OK, he didn't have any great work record. But he was good enough to fight in Kuwait. Why couldn't he catch a break just one time?

I was angry all the next day at school, which is probably why I ended up shooting off my mouth in Arnold's class. All week he'd been having us read famous speeches. Some I'd heard of, like Martin Luther King Jr.'s "I Have a Dream" speech, and Kennedy's Inaugural Address. Others, like Pericles' Funeral Oration, were new to me.

That day, he read us Lincoln's Gettysburg Address. Arnold has a radio-announcer's voice, and he used it. *"We here highly resolve,"* he said, reaching the end of the speech, *"that these dead shall not have died in vain—that this nation, under God, shall have a new birth of freedom—and that government of the people, by the people, for the people, shall not perish from the earth."*

There was a long moment of silence. Then Arnold closed the book and looked out over the class. "That speech is less than three hundred words long, but it is without doubt the greatest speech in American history, and one of the greatest speeches in world history."

"It's also a bunch of crap," I muttered, too loudly.

"What did you say?" Arnold asked, his eyes flaring in anger.

"Nothing," I said.

Heather Carp looked at me, and then at Arnold. "He said Lincoln's full of crap."

Arnold stiffened. "This is a classroom. I'd appreciate it if you'd use appropriate language."

"I didn't say Lincoln was full of crap, Mr. Arnold," Heather said, grinning. "He did."

The class laughed. Arnold turned to me.

"Explain what you mean, Chance."

"I didn't mean anything."

He glared at me. "You didn't mean anything. You sit in the back of the room and say nothing for weeks, and then you say Abraham Lincoln is full of crap, but you refuse to explain yourself. That's not going to cut it. I want you to tell me why you said what you did, and I want you to do it now."

I could feel everyone's eyes on me. Any other day and I would have just sat there until he gave up. But the anger I'd been carrying all day boiled over.

"You want to know what I mean?" I said. "OK, this is what I mean. It isn't rich kids getting killed in Iraq and Afghanistan, is it? It's not government of the people. It's government of the *rich* people. The poor get screwed over from the day they're born to the day they die."

As soon as I finished, I felt stupid. I should have kept my mouth shut. But Arnold didn't slap me down. Instead he took a deep breath, and when he exhaled the anger went out of his eyes. "That's a good point, Chance. It's something that needs to be discussed." He looked around the classroom. "Anyone care to comment on what Chance just said? Amy Yee, what do you think?"

I slipped down in my seat, and for the rest of class kept my eyes on my desk and my mouth shut while kids argued about whether it was right that mainly poor kids served in the army.

As I was heading out the door at the end of class, Arnold called me over. "You should raise your hand more often, Chance. That's the best discussion we've had in weeks."

CHAPTER FIFTEEN

When I finished my run that day, Melissa was waiting for me by the ramp leading down to Pier B. As soon as she saw me, she smiled and waved. "Hey, Chance."

I liked seeing her; I liked being near her. But not here, not by my boat. She was too close to things I didn't want anyone to know about. "What are you doing here, Melissa?"

"Nothing, really. I just wanted to talk to you."

"How did you find out where my boat is?"

She nodded toward the marina office. "They told me in there." She paused. "Is something wrong?"

"No. Nothing's wrong. I just wasn't expecting to see you."

She turned and faced the pier. "Which is your boat?"

"The *Tiny Dancer*," I said. "Slip forty-five." The boat was halfway down the pier. She looked, but I knew she couldn't pick it out.

"It must be neat living on a boat."

"It's OK," I said.

She wanted me to take her out onto the dock and show her the *Tiny Dancer*, but it was the last thing I'd ever do. Finally she turned away from the pier. "How about if we walk a little bit?" she said. "Maybe we could get some hot chocolate or something at Little Coney?"

"I don't have any money with me," I said, gesturing to my running clothes.

"My treat." She smiled. "Come on."

We walked toward Little Coney. For a time, neither of us spoke. "I've been thinking about what you said in class today," she said as we reached the yacht club building. "About how this is a country run by rich people."

"What about it?"

"My family is rich."

"I wasn't talking about your family, Melissa. I just meant rich people in general."

"But you're right, Chance. My older brothers are both at Yale. They aren't going into the army or the navy or anything like that. My mom would die if they enlisted."

"So?" I said.

"So if we were poor they might have to go someplace like Afghanistan or Iraq. Just like you said. And it's not right."

I stopped. "Melissa, I was just talking. Don't take everything so seriously."

"So I shouldn't pay attention to what you say?"

"No," I said. "You shouldn't."

She frowned, and we walked in silence the rest of the way. I pushed open the door to Little Coney and we stepped inside.

"Two hot chocolates," she said, putting money on the counter. We found a booth that looked out over the boat launch and sat down.

For a while we just drank our chocolate and looked at the water. Finally, Melissa broke the silence. Her voice was low, and she spoke slowly. "Did you know that your dad and my dad were best friends when they were kids? They both went to Ingraham High and played on the baseball team."

I stared at her, too stunned to answer.

She gave me a little smile. "I didn't think you did. I only found out because I mentioned your name at dinner after that whole thing with Brent Miller. My dad recognized it, and he showed me his old yearbooks. There had to be a half dozen pictures of your father and my father together. They were like brothers." She paused. "My dad says that your father was in the first Gulf War and that he saw a lot of action. Is that true?"

As soon as she mentioned the Gulf War, my throat tightened. I hated thinking about Melissa and her dad talking about us, feeling sorry for us. "Yeah, my dad fought in the Gulf War."

She tipped her cup this way and that way. "Look, Chance," she said at last. "My dad wanted me to tell you that if you or your dad ever need any help, he—"

"Melissa," I said, cutting her off, "we don't need your help."

She pushed her chocolate away from her. "I'm sorry, Chance. I didn't mean to hurt your feelings. I was just doing what my dad asked me to do."

"You didn't hurt my feelings," I said. "And it's nice of your father and all. But we don't need help. We're doing fine."

She nodded, and then she looked at her watch. "I should get going."

"I'll walk back with you," I said.

She stood. "No. Stay here. I'd rather walk alone."

CHAPTER SIXTEEN

It was a cold Friday afternoon one week later. I'd run my normal route, out to the locks, then back along the Shilshole marina through Golden Gardens Park and onto the beach toward Carkeek. I'd run fast, faster than ever. And the fast pace worked. For the last couple of miles I'd run the way an animal runs—pure motion and no thought. When I finally stopped running, it was as if I'd come out of a dream world. I wished I could have kept running forever.

But I couldn't, so I went down to the boat, grabbed some clean clothes, and headed back toward the bathroom at the end of the pier to shower. A cold wind was blowing off the Sound, and I felt a shiver go through me. As I started up the ramp toward the utility room and the showers, the fat guy from the marina office stepped from the sidewalk onto the ramp, blocking me.

He'd started working at the marina office toward the end of

summer. He was in charge of boats that needed temporary moorage. Charters, mainly. He liked to hang out on the sidewalk that ran between the parking lot and the piers, talking to people in a loud, know-it-all voice. Even on a gray, wet day he wore dark sunglasses and a Hawaiian shirt covered with birds and flowers. He had no neck; his bald head seemed to just sit on top of his shoulders.

"You run every day, kid?" he asked.

"What?" I said.

"You run every day?"

I shrugged. "Yeah. Pretty much."

He smiled. "Good for you. I like healthy kids. I wish I'd run when I was your age."

"I got to get going," I said, and I pushed by him.

"What's your hurry?" he said.

I kept going without looking back.

When I reached the utility room, I opened the door quickly, stepped inside, and pulled the heavy door shut. As usual the room was empty. I took the shower stall way in the back, turned the handles, and adjusted the water temperature. When it was hot, but not too hot, I undressed and stepped in. Then I closed my eyes and let the hot water pour over my head.

I was washing my hair when I heard the main door open. It creeps me out whenever that happens. I listened to hear if anyone was heading toward the shower stalls. Instead I heard the rumble of the clothes dryer as it started up. I rinsed the soap out of my hair, turned off the water, dried myself quickly, and dressed. While I was dressing, I heard the click of the main door as it closed. Whoever had come in was gone.

I gathered my dirty clothes together—the sound of the dryer reminded me I'd have to do a wash later. Then I combed my hair and headed back toward the locker area. When I rounded the corner, the fat guy was standing in front of the mirror, picking his teeth with a red toothpick. As soon as he saw me, he turned. "We weren't done talking."

I dropped my dirty clothes and curled my hands into fists. "You touch me, you pervert, and you'll pay for it."

He smiled. "Relax, kid. This has nothing to do with sex. I want to give you a chance to earn some easy money." He paused. "You need money, don't you?"

"No," I said. "I don't."

He tilted his head to the side and raised his eyebrows. "That's funny. Word at the office is that your old man lost his job over at Sunset West, that he missed his September payment, and that in a couple of months or so he's going to lose that beat-up sailboat you call home."

"My dad will get a job," I said.

He smiled. "You know something? I like your spirit. I really do. But I don't have time to play games. So listen, and listen carefully. You're in trouble, and I can get you out of that trouble. I'm offering you a job, kid. Very good pay; very short hours. When somebody offers you easy money, you should at least hear him out."

"I don't want easy money."

He smiled. "Is that right?" He reached into his pocket, pulled out a money clip, peeled off a one-hundred-dollar bill, and held it out to me. "It's your pay for hearing me out."

I stared at the money. He shook it. "Go on, take it. Otherwise I'm going to put it back in my pocket."

I reached out and took it. "All right," I said, sticking the bill in my back pocket. "I'll listen."

He looked around. "I think the sun came out. This isn't a good place to talk. How about we go for a walk?"

CHAPTER SEVENTEEN

We headed out onto the sidewalk that runs along the marina. For the first fifty yards or so, neither of us spoke. "OK," I said at last. "What do I have to do to earn this easy money?"

He stopped and leaned against the railing. "That's the beautiful part, kid. You just keep doing what you already do. Run. I'll pay you two hundred bucks a week to run."

"Come on," I said. "There's more to it than that."

He bobbed his fat head back and forth. "OK. Maybe there's a little more to it, but not much. Starting tomorrow, when you run you'll be wearing a backpack."

"A backpack?"

He shrugged. "You'll get used to it. People run with stuff all the time. Nobody will notice. You can stick a Walkman in it if you want, or a bottle of water. Do whatever you want—I don't care. Just so long as you wear it."

"So where do I run? And what's the backpack for?"

"The same route you always run. Out to the locks, over to Magnolia, back along the marina, through Golden Gardens Park, and then onto the beach."

"Have you been watching me?"

His eyes narrowed. "You bet I've been watching you. And I'll *be* watching you. This is business, kid." He stopped. An old couple was approaching, holding hands. Everything about them seemed relaxed, easy. The fat guy nodded to them. "Good afternoon."

"Good afternoon," the old man answered.

We watched them make their way leisurely down the sidewalk.

"You still haven't told me what I need the backpack for," I said when they were out of earshot.

"You know the tree that looks like it's growing out of the boulders? The big maple?"

He was talking about my mother's tree. "Sure. The train tracks are right above there. It's where I turn around."

"From now on, when you reach that tree, you'll stop and stretch, do some pushups, something. While you're doing whatever it is you do, you'll be looking hard into the nooks and crannies of the boulders around that tree."

"What'll I find?"

"Most days, nothing. But some days there will be a package. When there is, you slip the package into your backpack. Then you run back along the beach just like you normally would. You go down to your boat and get a change of clothes just like you always do. Then you come back up to the utility room at the end of the pier for a shower, same as usual. Before you shower, you stick the backpack in the locker. After you shower, you change into your clean clothes, stuff the dirty clothes into the backpack, but leave the package in the locker."

"Then what happens?"

"Then you do the same thing the next day."

"I mean, what happens to the packages? What's in them? Where do they go?"

He shook his head. "Bad questions. You don't know, and you don't want to find out. Understand?"

"This is drugs, isn't it? It's a smuggling operation."

"Didn't you hear me? You don't know and you don't want to know. All you need to know is what I've told you."

"I'm not getting involved in drugs," I said.

"You're the one saying drugs and smuggling. All I'm talking about is running on the beach and picking up packages."

"I'm not doing it," I said.

"You're going to lose your boat. You know that, don't you?" I didn't answer.

He shook his head and smiled. "You're a pain in the ass, kid. A real pain in the ass. I'm throwing you and your old man a life preserver and you won't grab hold. But I'm a patient man, so here's what I'll do for you. You think over my offer this weekend. On Monday, you'll find a gray backpack in your locker. If you wear that backpack when you run, I'll know you want the job. If you don't wear it, I'll find somebody who knows a good deal when he sees one."

"How are you going to get into my locker?" I said. "You don't know my combination."

He reached into his pocket and pulled out a key chain filled with keys. "Don't forget. I work here. I've got keys to everything." Then he smiled, turned on his heels, and walked away.

Once I was back on the *Tiny Dancer*, I took the hundred-dollar bill out and held it up to the light. I don't know why—it's not as if I could recognize a counterfeit bill, anyway. Then I laid it on the table and stared at it.

If you live on the waterfront long enough, you know illegal stuff goes on. You don't see it necessarily, but you feel it—people that don't look quite right, boats that don't look quite right. The Coast Guard and the port police aren't there for the fun of it. Twice in the last year I'd seen guys get arrested at the marina.

The fat man knew more than he was letting on, that was for sure. If the whole thing were as easy as he said it was, he wouldn't pay me for doing it. He'd take a stroll down the beach after work and pick up the packages himself. There was no future in what he was proposing, but I wasn't worried about the future. I was worried about next month. I picked up the bill and held it to the light again.

CHAPTER EIGHTEEN

The next day was a Saturday—and that meant work. At one-forty-five I headed up Seaview Avenue toward Ray's. You hear about restaurants having filthy kitchens but Creager ran that kitchen as if it were a hospital. "Spic and span!" he'd say every time he walked through. "Clean and cleaner!"

I hated everything about my job: the windowless room, the food baked on the pans, the smell of the soap. But most of all I hated the heat. To satisfy Creager, the water had to be just short of boiling. I wore rubber gloves that went up to my elbows, but I could still feel the heat right through them. No matter how cold it was outside, I always stripped down to a T-shirt and shorts when I worked. Even so, I'd be sweating like a pig within five minutes of starting my shift.

I scrubbed those pots until they shined, then scrubbed them some more. After that I rinsed them over and over. The first day I'd worked there, I sent a pan to the cooks that hadn't been rinsed enough. "Do you eat soap?" Creager had screamed, holding the pan up. "Do you?" When I shook my head, he got right up in my face. "Well, neither do our customers. Never send back a pan like this again. Do you hear me?"

I worked Saturday and Sunday that weekend, from two in the afternoon until ten at night. Through both shifts, all I could think about was the hundred-dollar bill the fat guy had given me. Eight bucks an hour is what I made at Ray's. But I didn't get all eight dollars. After the government took out all the stuff they take out of paychecks, I took home less than seven an hour. Sixteen hours of hard work for what the fat guy had given me to listen to him talk.

Creager came over to me as I was hanging up my apron at the end of my shift on Sunday night. "I won't be needing you until four o'clock from now on, Chance. I'm sorry. I really am. I know things are tough for you and your dad. Around Christmas, business is sure to pick up. When it does, I'll get you more hours. And if anything comes up for your dad over the holidays, I'll let you know."

"Don't worry about me," I said. "I've got a line on another job. The pay is better and so is the work. I'm sick of scrubbing pots, anyway."

Creager stiffened. "When will you know about this new job?"

"I already know about it," I said.

"So when will you be quitting here?"

I hung my apron on the little hook and turned to him.

"That's it. I'm done."

"You sure?"

"I'm sure."

As I walked back to the *Tiny Dancer* that night, the cool evening air somehow didn't cool me. I felt light in the head and wobbly in the knees. I thought about the kids at school, about Melissa. What would they say, what would she say, if they found out that Chance Taylor, the guy in the back of the classroom who never said anything, was a drug smuggler?

PART TWO

CHAPTER ONE

As soon as school ended on Monday, I hustled down to the boat and changed into my running clothes. A couple of minutes later I was standing in front of my locker in the utility room, my hands sweating. Finally, I worked the combination and opened it. Inside was a small gray backpack. I stared at it for a while as if it were a bomb before finally picking it up. I pulled the backpack over my shoulders and adjusted the shoulder straps. I took a deep breath and then headed off at my normal pace down Seaview Avenue toward the Ballard Locks.

As I ran, I passed a middle-aged lady wearing a pink Adidas sweat suit with matching wristbands and headband. Next an old guy on a girl's bike rolled by, his black poodle panting to keep up. Two bicyclists flew by on the other side of the street; both were wearing black spandex shorts and canary-yellow shirts. Outside the Juice House a college guy was talking on a cell phone, a ferret under his arm. The fat guy had been right: nobody was going to notice my backpack.

I did a quick loop through the gardens at the locks, and then retraced my steps, running down Seaview and past Pier B. At the end of the marina, I entered Golden Gardens Park. I ran across the grassy fields—packed with kite fliers and dog walkers in the summer but empty now—and along the boardwalk by the duck ponds until I reached the beach. A good wind was coming out of the north; the wind and sand made the running hard.

When I reached the maple tree, I stopped. I put my hands flat against the trunk and stretched my hamstrings. It was a natural enough thing to do and a natural enough place to do it; I'd often stretched there. But this time my heart raced as my eyes furiously scanned the nooks and crannies in the big rocks that served as a retaining wall for the railroad tracks.

And then, there it was: a black plastic bag stuck between two rocks. My hand was trembling as I reached in and pulled the bag out. Inside was a small brown package, about the size of a shoe box, weighing between five and ten pounds.

I shoved the trash bag and the package into the backpack, hurriedly zipped it shut, and then turned around. Walking toward me was a man who, for a split second, I thought was Mr. Arnold. I froze, and then watched as he threw a stick into the Sound. His big black dog bounded into the water after it. "Loves to swim, that one," the man said, and I saw that he didn't look like Arnold at all. I nodded, and then broke into a jog and started back.

When I reached Pier B, I stopped and walked. My dad, for

the first afternoon in weeks, was onboard. He was sitting in the cabin looking at his charts. I grabbed clean clothes from the storage bin under the bench. "I'm going to shower up," I said.

He looked up. "I'll probably be gone when you get back," he said. If he noticed the backpack, he didn't say anything.

Once I was in the utility room, I shoved the backpack into my locker and carried my clothes to the shower stall. I stuck them and my towel on top of the dressing bench to keep them from getting wet, and then I took a long shower. The whole time I listened for the main door to open, but I didn't hear a thing. When I finished showering, I dried myself and dressed. I couldn't leave without knowing, so I again opened the combination lock and peered inside. The backpack and the package were still there, exactly the way I'd left them.

Back on the sailboat, I was all nerves. I kept thinking about the package, wondering who would pick it up and when. I tried listening to the radio, but I couldn't get my mind off the backpack. Finally I walked the length of the marina just to be doing something. The whole time I was out, nothing seemed to be out of the ordinary. Just another night at the marina. I finally went back to the boat.

It wasn't until eleven that I flicked off the light and tried to sleep, but that was no good either. When my dad came in a little after one, I was wide awake. I fell asleep sometime around two, but even then I slept fitfully, waking up every hour or so, wondering if somehow something had gone wrong.

I was up before six Tuesday morning. I poured myself a bowl of cereal and took it up on deck to get away from my dad. Some of the other live-aboards were stirring, but the marina was basically quiet. Instead of eating, I stepped off the boat and walked the length of the pier and up the ramp toward the utility room.

The whole time I kept thinking about the locker and the package and the fat guy, and the more I thought, the more certain I became that something had gone wrong. I turned the key to the utility room door and then worked the combination to my locker. Once I heard the *click*, I opened the door. The backpack was there, but the package was gone.

When I came out, the fat guy was leaning against the wall of the utility room, smoking a cigarette. He smiled when he saw me. "Let's walk," he said.

We headed toward Little Coney. "I'm going to make this quick. You get paid every Sunday—the money will be in the front pouch of your backpack. If you see me on the marina, you can nod to me or you can ignore me. I don't care. What you can't do is come into the marina office to talk to me. If we need to talk, I'll come to you. Understood?"

"Understood," I said.

"Good." He smiled. "You're not as dumb as I thought you were, and now you're going to be a whole lot richer."

CHAPTER TWO

I wasn't playing a game. This was for real. This was dangerous. Smugglers got busted; smugglers did time in prison. Sometimes, smugglers got themselves killed. I knew it, but somehow I couldn't make myself believe it.

Maybe that's because for a while, nothing happened. Every day I'd run. Every day I'd stop by the big maple and do some stretches. Every day my eyes scanned the nooks and crannies of the rocks. Every day I reached my hand into the deeper recesses and felt around in there. And every day there'd be nothing. Absolutely nothing. There was no package the next day, or the day after, or that whole week.

I got paid, just the way the fat man said I would be. And no packages meant no danger, or at least less danger, so I should have been happy, but I wasn't. I was counting on that money, and I knew nobody was going to keep paying me two hundred dollars a week to do nothing.

At school the following Thursday, the only things I could think about were the fat guy and the rocks and the package and money. By the time school ended, all I wanted to do was run out to the rocks. But when I stepped onto the boat, my dad was waiting for me.

"Put your stuff away, Chance. We're going to the food bank."

"Now?" I said.

"Yeah, now."

"I can't. I've got to run now."

"What do you mean you've got to run now? You can run anytime. Store your stuff down below and let's get going. The bus comes in five minutes."

We caught the bus on Seaview and got off at Twenty-fourth and Market. It started to drizzle as we began the twelve-block walk to the North End Emergency Center. "I think I'm close to having enough money to pay October's moorage fees," I said as we trudged up the hill.

"How?" he said.

"I've got a new job."

He looked over at me. "You quit Ray's?"

I nodded. "I'm picking up and delivering stuff now."

"What stuff?"

"Packages. I get tips too. If you've got any money, we could put it together and probably make it."

My dad thought for a while as we walked. "It'd be good to pay," he said at last. "Keep them off our backs." He put his hand out. "Give me what you got."

A chill passed through me. "I've only gotten one paycheck," I said. I paused. "How about you give what you've got to me, and I'll take care of it?"

He didn't answer. Instead, he lit a cigarette and started walking again. When we reached the food bank, he reached into his back pocket and pulled out his wallet. He counted out six old, ragged twenty-dollar bills and handed them to me. The other twenties—I couldn't tell whether there were two or three—he kept. He caught me looking at them. "A man needs some money in his wallet," he said. Then he pulled open the door to the food bank, and I followed him inside.

CHAPTER THREE

By the door stood a silver-haired guy, neatly dressed in a sport coat and slacks, but not wearing a tie. "Good afternoon," he said, smiling as if we were customers at the supermarket. "Boxes are to your left."

Four other people were there—three women and a homeless guy. Two of the women and the man acted just like Dad and me. They moved up and down the aisles picking out spaghetti noodles, cans of soup, jars of peanut butter—stuff like that. They kept their heads down and their mouths shut. But the woman wearing the Washington State Cougar sweatshirt was different. "You got any other crackers besides these?" she called out to the man in front.

"All we have is what's out," the man called back to her.

"How about cookies, then? My girls like Oreos, and I don't see even one package of Oreos."

"Everything we have is on the shelves," the man repeated.

"You must have more stuff somewhere. You hiding it from us?"

My dad and I filled our boxes quickly. "Thanks," my dad said as we headed out the door.

"We'll be open Tuesday and Thursday next week. Regular hours."

The boxes were too heavy to carry the twelve blocks to Market Street. There was nothing to do but wait for the bus, take it to Market, and then transfer to the bus to the marina. It had taken an hour already; it looked like it might take another hour to return.

My dad sat down inside the bus shelter, but I was too nervous to sit. Every few minutes I'd take a step into the street to see if I could spot the bus. I needed to get back. I needed to run. I needed to check the rocks.

When I stepped out for what must have been the tenth time, a blue Jetta came over the crest of the hill. I stepped back onto the sidewalk, but Melissa had spotted me. As she drove past, she tapped lightly on the horn and waved. I managed to wave back.

She turned right at the corner and was gone. Two minutes later I again stepped into the street to look for the bus. But instead of the bus, there was the blue Jetta again. This time Melissa pulled over and rolled down the window. "You need a ride?"

Before I could turn her down, my dad stood up. "We sure do, young lady," he called, smiling broadly and picking up the box of groceries at his feet.

Melissa smiled back. "You can put the groceries in the

trunk," she said, and she reached down to pull the lever that popped open the trunk of the car.

My dad quickly put his box in the trunk. I picked up the second box and loaded it as well. My dad climbed into the back seat, as if he were a little kid, while Melissa and I sat in the front. "I didn't know there was a grocery store around here," she said as she pulled into traffic.

"There isn't," I replied.

I knew what I'd said made no sense to her, but she let it go.

"You going to your boat?"

I nodded.

She drove down to Market and made the turn toward the marina. I wanted to say something, but my mind was blank. In the back seat my father sat staring out the window.

Just after she drove past the Ballard Locks, the sailboats moored in the marina came into view. Behind them was Puget Sound, gray like the sky, and deep in the clouds were the Olympic Mountains.

"It's so beautiful here," Melissa said. "I keep meaning to come down here and run along the water." She paused. "You still run, don't you?"

"Sometimes," I said.

"What are you talking about?" my father said from the back. "You run every day."

"You can let us off up there," I said, pointing to an empty parking spot.

"Shouldn't I pull up closer to the pier?"

"There's never any parking by the pier. This is great."

She came to a stop, and then reached down to pull the lever to open the trunk.

"Thanks for the ride," I said, stepping out of the car.

"See you tomorrow," she answered.

"Yeah. See you tomorrow."

"Thanks," my dad said.

"I'm Melissa Watts," she said then, leaning back and shaking his hand. "You and my dad went to Ingraham High together. Trevor Watts. Do you remember him?"

His eyes widened. "Sure," he said. "I remember Trevor."

"Come on, Dad," I said, before he could say more. "Let's get these boxes onto the boat."

CHAPTER FOUR

We lugged the groceries across the parking lot, down the ramp, and onto the sailboat. Below deck, we unpacked and stored all the cans of food. I slid open the front panel of the storage nook where I kept my running clothes. "I'm going to run now."

"Take a day off, Chance," he said. "How about if you and me eat a normal meal for once? I could cook some soup. This bread is actually fresh."

"I can't."

"What do you mean you can't?"

"I just can't. Besides, I'm not hungry."

The drizzle had turned to rain and the sky was a gloomy gray. I opened the locker in the utility room, slung the backpack over my shoulders, and stepped outside. If I ran all the way out to the locks, it would be dark by the time I returned to the beach. So instead of running my normal route, I headed straight out to the beach.

By the time I reached the big tree, twilight was giving way to night. I stretched, looking as carefully as I could into the shadows of the rocks. Nothing—but it was too dark to really see. I turned and checked the beach in both directions. No one. I stopped pretending I was stretching, and instead reached into the openings in the rocks to feel around for a package. Still nothing. If only I'd brought a flashlight.

I ran back along the beach, showered as usual, and then returned to the boat. My dad was gone; an unopened can of soup and a clean bowl sat on the small table.

That night I lay awake thinking. I saw myself back on the beach feeling around the rocks with my hands, only now I'd find something, something I'd missed. The sensation was so strong I almost dressed and returned to the beach to look again.

Friday morning, as I crossed the marina parking lot on my way to school, the fat guy hopped out of a silver Acura I hadn't noticed. He grabbed me by the elbow and pulled me to a fenced area full of garbage dumpsters and recycling bins. "I ran yesterday," I said straight away. "I swear I did. There was nothing there."

"How come I didn't see you, then?"

"I had to help my dad when I got home from school," I said. "Since I was late, I took a shortcut. It was almost dark, but I checked. I swear to God there was nothing there."

"It was there, all right. It's still there. You missed it."

"I'll go right now," I said, and I started toward the beach.

He grabbed me and pulled me back. "You'll go at the regular time." He reached into his back pocket and pulled out a small card. He wrote something on the back of it and then handed it to me. "You call that number if you are ever going to miss a pickup."

"Who do I ask for?"

"You don't ask for anybody. It's an answering machine. At the beep, you leave a message—'Chance is out of the race today.' You understand?"

"Yeah," I said. "I understand."

"There's money in this for both of us. Don't blow it."

The package was the size of a loaf of bread. It was wedged between two rocks; the day before, my hands must have gone just under it. I dislodged it, and then shoved it into my backpack. When I turned around, a little beagle was running toward me, his nose on the ground. A woman about thirty was twenty feet behind him. The dog started barking at me. "That dog should be on a leash," I shouted.

"I'm sorry," she said. Then she started calling her dog. "Come here, Flip. Come on, boy."

I kept a steady pace on the run back to the pier, the package thumping against my back. It was awkward, but I didn't care. I had my job.

There was another package hidden in the rocks Saturday. On Sunday afternoon in the front pouch of the backpack I found a sealed envelope. Inside were four fifty-dollar bills.

CHAPTER FIVE

October 31—Halloween. When I got home from school, my dad was sitting on deck wearing his heavy parka and reading the newspaper. It was cold and drizzly; he should have been in the cabin. But when I went down below, I understood why he wanted to stay outside. On the navigation table was the bill for the moorage fee. I grabbed it and climbed back up.

"You got enough money?" he said.

"Yeah. I got enough."

"And next month?"

"I'll have enough to pay for everything."

"Even food?"

"I think so."

"So you don't need your old man anymore for anything, do you?"

"I'm going to go to the office and pay this," I said, holding up the piece of paper. "I'll see you later."

When I reached the marina office, I pushed open the glass door and stepped inside. The fat guy was sitting at a desk in the back. Our eyes caught, but I didn't nod and neither did he. A fiftyish woman stood behind the counter. "Can I help you?" she said.

I pulled the paper out of my back pocket and laid it on the counter. "I'm here to pay the moorage fee. Pier B, slip forty-five. Taylor is the last name. I know we're a month behind, but I'll be paying that soon too." I opened my wallet and counted out two hundred and eighty dollars.

Instead of picking the money up, the woman just stared at it. "What's wrong?" I said.

She looked up at me. "Oh, sorry. Nothing's wrong. It's just that most people drop a check into the collection box outside the door." She smiled and picked up the bills. "But cash is perfectly OK. I'll write you a receipt and get you your change."

She went into a little glass cubicle. I could see her talking to a man in there. He looked out at me, and then said something to her. A minute later she came out.

"Thanks," I said after she'd counted out twelve dollars and given me a receipt.

Stupid, I thought as I stepped out. The first chance I got, I'd open a checking account. Next month, I'd write a check and drop the fee in the box, like regular people did. I had to be careful. Very careful. I had to make sure nothing I did looked suspicious.

CHAPTER SIX

I was a criminal, involved in a smuggling ring, but the amazing thing was how quickly it became routine. My heart didn't pound anymore when I reached the maple tree. I took my time when I stretched so I could look carefully in the rocks. Most days there was nothing. But every three or four days, there'd be a package.

I was pretty sure I had the basics of the operation figured out. Boats come into Puget Sound all the time. If a boat is from Canada or China or some other foreign country, the captain has to call a customs agent and somebody from immigration. Maybe the boat gets checked thoroughly and maybe it doesn't. But getting drugs off the boat before any possible inspection would be the smart thing to do, just in case. It would be easy to slip someone to shore at night, store the drugs in the rocks, and then have that person return to the boat.

The smugglers probably used the same boat over and

over—most likely some sort of charter boat that was familiar enough to Coast Guard patrols that they left it alone. The captain could do the smuggling without the owner of the boat even knowing about it. Or some crewman could be doing it without the captain knowing—though that would be less likely. In middle school, the D.A.R.E. cop told us that on the street an ounce of marijuana could sell for as much as a hundred bucks. The packages I was carrying weighed between five and ten pounds, which would translate into over ten thousand dollars. At two shipments a week, the total value would be more than a million dollars a year. If cocaine were ever in those packages, the street value would be even more. No wonder they could pay me two hundred bucks a week.

I wasn't sure how the fat guy figured in. Maybe he was a big player in the deal—the guy who got the drugs to the street. Maybe he was a small fry who'd fallen into some easy money. Sometimes I wanted to find out what happened to the packages after I stuck them in the locker, but then I'd remember what the fat man had said about knowing too much, and I let it drop.

The Monday before Thanksgiving vacation, the counselors set up Career Day in the commons area. People from the University of Washington and Seattle University and Shoreline College and a bunch of other schools stood behind tables and passed out brochures.

I didn't even bother to look at the college brochures—what point was there? When I finished eating lunch, I walked across the commons to the back door. That's where I spotted

Melissa toe-to-toe with Ms. Dugan, the vice principal. The two of them were standing in front of a table manned by an armed forces recruiter with a grim smile on his face. I hadn't noticed either the table or the guy, that's how deep in the corner they were.

I stopped about ten feet from Melissa. She had on her Stanford sweatshirt and jeans. Her face was bright red, and so was Dugan's. They were talking in low voices, but anybody could see they were both angry.

While they were arguing, some kid I didn't know pushed past Melissa and approached the recruiter's table. Melissa spun around. "Don't believe a word he says," she yelled so loudly that everyone in the commons turned to stare at her. Melissa paused and then pointed at the recruiter. "He'll get you killed if you let him!"

"That's enough of that!" Dugan broke in angrily. "More than enough. If you don't leave here right now, Melissa Watts, I am going to call security and have you removed."

Melissa glowered at Dugan.

"Did you hear me? Either you leave or security comes and makes you leave."

"I have a constitutional right to say whatever I want."

"You are on school property, Melissa, and you do not have the right to disrupt educational activities."

"Oh, so signing up to get killed is an *educational* activity!"

I pushed my way up to Melissa. "Let's get out of here, Melissa," I said. "Fifth period is about to begin, anyway." Melissa looked at me and then at Dugan. "It's not worth it," I whispered.

She turned back to Dugan. "I'm leaving," she said. "But not because of you. I'm leaving because I want to leave."

"I don't care why you leave," Dugan said. "Just leave."

Melissa shook free of me, turned her back, and strode out of the commons. Ms. Dugan followed a few seconds later. I started to walk away when the recruiter called out, "Hey, you." I turned back. He shoved a brochure into my hand. "Do me a favor. Stick this in your pocket and look at it over sometime."

After Arnold's class ended, Melissa walked to the locker bay with me. "It makes me mad they allow those guys on campus," she said, still fixated on her lunchtime face-off with Dugan. "It's just wrong."

"Come on, Melissa. There are worse things than joining the army."

"Yeah?" she said. "Name one."

"Going to jail," I said.

She laughed mockingly. "As if that's an option."

I'd reached my locker. She watched as I spun the dial on my lock. "I appreciate what you did, Chance. That's the second time you've been there for me."

"I didn't do anything."

"Yes, you did. I don't need anything bad on my record, not if I'm going to get into Stanford. And being hauled off by security is definitely bad."

"They wouldn't have hauled you off."

"Dugan would have loved to call security. She's never liked me."

I slammed my locker shut and turned. "I've got to go, Melissa." I started toward the exit.

"Wait—can I ask you something, Chance?"

I turned back. "Ask whatever you want."

"What are you looking for in those rocks?"

It was the last thing I was expecting her to say. I could feel the blood start to pound in my temples. "What are you talking about?" I said, trying to keep my face from going red.

"The rocks below the railroad tracks. When you run, you stop and look around."

"Are you spying on me?"

"No," she said.

"How do you know what I do or don't do, then?" I said.

"Chance, I do my homework in our solarium, which looks out over the beach. I've seen you a couple of times now, poking around in the rocks. That's all. If I'd known you were going to get all paranoid, I wouldn't have mentioned it. I was just curious."

"I'm not paranoid, Melissa. I just don't like being spied on."

She stared at me for a long moment. "Forget I mentioned it," she said.

CHAPTER SEVEN

'd been an idiot to snarl at Melissa like that. All I'd done was make her more suspicious. If the fat guy knew someone was watching me, he'd get rid of me. I couldn't have that, not when things had fallen into place. Creager wouldn't take me back at Ray's.

When I reached the maple tree that day, I looked up at the homes along the bluff. Back in middle school, someone had pointed out Melissa's house to me from the road, but I couldn't pick it out from the beach. Was she in her solarium—whatever that was—right now? Was she watching me?

There was nothing hidden in the rocks that day, so I turned and headed back. When I reached Pier B, I spotted a huge water rat cleaning itself on the rocks. The rat looked at me, and then went right back to cleaning itself. That rat gave me an idea.

Tuesday before school I tracked down Melissa. "I'm sorry about yesterday," I said.

"Forget it," she said, her voice icy.

"It's a rat's nest," I said.

"What?"

"In the rocks. There's a bunch of paper and wrappers all in a mound. I think a momma rat and her babies live in there. Sometimes I can see little pink eyes looking back at me."

Her eyes brightened. "That's cool. Why didn't you just say so?"

"I don't know. I guess I thought you'd think it was stupid."

"Well, I don't. I think it's nice."

For a moment we both stood there. "See you around," I said at last, and started off.

"Chance, wait a second," she said.

I stopped. "What?"

"That's the kind of thing you could write about."

"What?"

"For the newspaper. You could write about stuff that goes on along Golden Gardens and on the beach. The rats, or something else if you want." She paused. "The newspaper staff still meets at the Blue Note Café at eight o'clock every other Friday. Our next meeting is this Friday. Why don't you come?"

I started to say no automatically, but then I stopped myself. For the first time in my life, I had money in my pocket. Not a lot, but enough so that I could buy a mocha and a piece of cake and not worry about it. I liked Melissa, and she liked me. She was just asking me to meet her at a café. How could going to the Blue Note hurt?

"OK," I said.

She smiled. "OK."

CHAPTER EIGHT

The first few years we lived on the boat, my dad would heat up some sort of turkey loaf and deli mashed potatoes for Thanksgiving. Some years, he even bought a pumpkin pie. He was trying, but all he did was to make me feel mom's absence even more.

Now we basically treat Thanksgiving and Christmas and birthdays as if they are any other day of the week. Since there's no buildup, there's no letdown. Thanksgiving came and went.

The morning after Thanksgiving, my dad gave me a hundred and thirty dollars. "To help with the moorage fee," he said. "I've had a few jobs lately. Mainly helping guys get their boats ready for winter."

I was about to tell him I didn't need it, but I stopped myself in time. "Thanks," I said. "This will help a lot."

That evening, after he'd taken off for wherever it was he

was going, I grabbed a jacket and walked the length of the marina to the long stairway leading up to Thirty-second Avenue and the Blue Note Café. It's about one hundred steps, straight up, so I was breathing hard when I finally reached the top.

I caught my breath, then crossed the street and entered the café. Melissa, her brown, shoulder-length hair pulled into a short ponytail, was sitting at a table in the back. She waved and I walked back to meet her. "You know Thomas Dowell and Annie Comstock, don't you?"

"Sure," I said, though I hadn't spoken ten words to either of them the whole time I'd been at Lincoln. "Good to see you."

Thomas and Annie had already bought their food, so I was able to go to the front counter with Melissa. "A large mocha and a scone," she said to the girl taking orders.

"I'll have the same," I said.

We stood side by side as the girl put our order together. "I'm really glad you came," Melissa said. "I didn't think you would."

"I wasn't sure I would, either."

"I know most people think the newspaper is nerdy and all that, but it really isn't."

Before I had to answer, the order came up. "I'll pay," I said, taking out my wallet.

"You pay for yours and I'll pay for mine," Melissa said.

"No," I said. "You bought at Little Coney. I'm paying this time."

We carried our food back to the table. While we'd been gone, Natasha Martin had joined the others. "I can only stay for a little while," she said. "My cousin from North Carolina is visiting. He got accepted into Harvard last week. Fifteen-fifty on the SAT. My parents want me to talk to him. As if talking about the SAT can help me score higher. I'll be lucky to get into Central Washington."

"You'll get into a good school," Melissa said. "You know you will."

For the next half hour, they talked about colleges. One place was great for pre-law while another had a fantastic biology program. Some other place had a sister school in Istanbul and another one had a junior-year program in Paris. Most of the schools they mentioned I'd never heard of. Occasionally Melissa would look over at me and smile.

I'd always thought that if I had a few bucks in my pocket, I'd be even with kids like Melissa and Thomas and Annie and Natasha. Now I had money, probably more money than anyone else at the table, but it didn't even things up at all. They were still them, and I was still me.

"Maybe we should talk about the newspaper," Melissa said at last. "That's why we're here, isn't it?"

Thomas groaned. "Couldn't we just skip it?"

Melissa shook her head. "Chance came because he's interested in joining the staff."

"That's OK," I muttered. "Talk about whatever you want to talk about."

Thomas smiled. "See, Melissa. He doesn't care."

"Well, I do," Melissa said. "And I'm the editor. So let's get to the meeting."

Melissa told them about the rats living in the rocks. She looked to Thomas. "Maybe you could take some pictures and Chance could write it up?"

I panicked, but Thomas saved me. "I don't want to get into cutesy-bunny-and-kitten crap. That sort of stuff is for the Wednesday shopper." He looked at me. "No offense, Chance."

Melissa sighed. "All right. Anybody else have any ideas for Chance? Something to do with the waterfront?"

"How about if he writes about the seals in the harbor?" Annie said. "The ones that are eating all the salmon and ruining the salmon runs."

"That's old news," Melissa said. "The *Times* has had about fifty articles about that."

"He could write about the threat of terrorism," Natasha said.

"What threat of terrorism?" Melissa asked.

"My dad has a friend who works for the FBI. He says they're really worried about the ports. There are zillions of boats floating around on the Sound and nobody keeps track of them. Terrorists could sail in and blow up whatever they wanted."

Melissa looked at me. "Is that true?"

"I wouldn't say nobody keeps track," I said. "There's the Coast Guard and the port police, and there's customs and there's immigration. Homeland Security must be down there too, but I don't think I've ever seen them."

"But they don't check all the boats, do they?" Natasha insisted.

"No," I said. "How could they?"

Thomas snorted in disgust. "I can see the headline now: *Terrorists at Shilshole! A* Lincoln Light *Exclusive.*"

"What's so ridiculous about it?" Natasha snapped. "It's not impossible that terrorists could come through Shilshole."

"And if they do, reporters from the *Lincoln Light* will be there to catch them!" Thomas said. He turned to Melissa. "I bet Stanford will admit you if you win a Pulitzer."

"Very funny, Thomas," Melissa said, and then she turned to me. "It isn't a bad idea, Chance. It really isn't. You don't have to find real terrorists or anything like that. All you have to do is write about how easy it would be for terrorists to get into the marina. It's worth thinking about."

"OK, he can think about it," Thomas said, interrupting. "And while he's thinking about it, I'll write the end-of-season wrap-up for soccer, volleyball, and football. But you've got to get the newspaper out before Christmas break, Melissa, or it will all be dumb. You know that, don't you?"

"I know it," Melissa said. "And it will come out before Christmas. I guarantee it."

Natasha looked at her watch. "Oh my God," she said. "I was supposed to be home thirty minutes ago."

I saw my chance. "I've got to go, too."

"Get down there and check the docks, Chance," Thomas said. "Some terrorist might be sailing in tonight with a nuclear bomb. You wouldn't want to miss that."

"You're not funny, Thomas," Melissa said. She stood and turned to me. "I'll go out with you."

Outside, the night air was cold. She walked across the street with me to the top of the stairway. "Don't pay any attention to Thomas," she said. "That's just how he is. You will write something, won't you?"

I shrugged. "About what?"

"You could write about the salmon runs. It is important, even if it's not new. I won't be able to get a newspaper out by Christmas if I don't get some stories soon."

CHAPTER NINE

It was too early to go to sleep, and I didn't feel like reading or watching television or listening to the radio. I ended up cleaning useless stuff out of my school backpack and from my storage nooks. That's how I came across the army brochure the recruiter had given me on Career Day.

I threw it right into the trash with a bunch of other papers, but then I reached in and pulled it back out. Melissa, Thomas, Annie, Natasha—all of them were moving on with their lives. They were heading to college; the world was getting larger for them. Where was I going? What was I going to do?

I flipped through the glossy pages. It was pure marketing. I knew from my dad that the army was nothing like the brochure pretended. Nothing like it at all. And I was no big patriot either. Still, it wasn't the *Tiny Dancer*. It wasn't smuggling and it wasn't Ray's restaurant and it wasn't a hundred other crummy jobs I could see myself doing. At the end, there'd be money for college, though I didn't know what I'd study at college if I ever got there.

The next morning I went to the pay phone by the marina building and made the call. The man at the other end was businesslike. The first thing he did was ask my name.

"My name," I said, stumbling for words.

"Yes, your name."

"My name is Todd Jones."

"And how old are you, Todd?"

"I'll be eighteen in August," I said.

"Are you enrolled in high school?"

"This is my last year."

"Will you graduate?"

"I guess," I said. "I'm passing everything. I'm not any great student, though."

"That's all right. We'd like you to graduate before you enlist, though it's not required. How about if we schedule an appointment? I can show you your various options, get a feel for the programs that might interest you."

My mouth went dry. "What I really want to know is how long would it take? I mean, from the time I signed the papers until I got in."

"Not long. Ten days if you're in a big hurry and you're not fussy about your program. Longer if there's a particular program you want or if you want to do a few things before you enlist."

"As fast as ten days?" I said.

"As fast as ten days." He paused. "It's a great opportunity. You'll get a chance to grow up, a chance to learn something about yourself and the world. And when your enlistment is finished, you'll be eligible for up to fifty thousand dollars for your college education. But really, it would be better if you came in so that I could show you the various enlistment options and go over the benefits that come with each. Do you want to schedule an appointment?"

"Right now I'm just thinking things over," I said. "I'll call back another time."

"That's fine. But before you call, I want you to think about what it means to be a soldier. Defending your country will require courage. There is no place for a coward in the armed forces."

"I know that," I said. "And I'm not a coward. If I was a coward, I wouldn't even call."

"Good. I'm glad to hear it. So the next time you call, I'll be expecting you to use your real name."

CHAPTER TEN

The strange envelope showed up in early December. It was a standard size, probably nine by twelve, but the paper was darker and felt rougher to the fingers than any envelope I'd seen in stores in Seattle. In the upper right-hand corner was a long string of numbers. The 7s had that little line in the middle of them that Europeans use, and the 1s had loops in front of them that made them look like 7s.

I was fingering the envelope, wondering if I should even take it, when I heard a woman laugh. I looked up the beach and saw a whole group of women jogging toward me. I shoved the envelope into my backpack and started back for the marina. When I reached the utility room, I stuck the envelope into the locker the same way I did the regular packages.

Melissa had been on me about writing something for the newspaper. I didn't want to let her down, so that night I went to the Ballard library and looked up salmon in an encyclopedia. I copied down stuff about how they spawn and how seals and dams and pollution are ruining everything. For about twenty minutes I wrote.

When I'd filled a couple of notebook pages, I stopped and read it over. Right away I knew it was all wrong. Melissa didn't want me to write a school report. She wanted something lively, something interesting. But what did I have to say about salmon or seals that would be lively or interesting? I ripped up the pages, tossed them into the trash, and started for home.

Outside in the night air, I found myself thinking about that envelope again. What could it have been? It was too light and too flat to contain drugs; I was sure of that. But if it was just some papers, why not stick them in the mail? Why go through all the trouble of hiding papers in rocks? It didn't make sense.

Instead of boarding the sailboat when I reached the marina, I returned to the utility room. I wanted to look at the envelope again. As I turned the key in the lock, I had a strange feeling I was being watched. I looked around quickly—no one. I pushed the utility room door open. As usual, the room was empty. I went to my locker, opened it, reached in for the envelope, but it was gone.

I closed the locker and headed back outside. As I stepped out onto the sidewalk, the bright lights of a car blinded me. I put my arm up to shield my eyes. The driver sped toward me, and then veered off hard to the right, tires squealing. As the car sped off, I got a good look at it. It was a newer-model black Mercedes, but the windows were so heavily tinted I couldn't tell how many people were inside.

My heart was racing, and so was my mind. Once I was back on the sailboat, with the security gate between me and the parking lot, I took a series of deep breaths to calm myself. It was dumb to be afraid. The driver of the Mercedes was probably some kid my age working as a valet at one of the fancy restaurants down the road, maybe even Ray's. It was just a coincidence that he sped up as I opened the door, nothing more. I was making a whole lot out of nothing.

CHAPTER ELEVEN

That Friday night I trudged up the hill to meet Melissa and the others at the Blue Note Café. I was late, but when I stepped through the door into the warmth of the coffee shop, the only person I saw was Melissa. She was drinking a latte and picking at a biscotti. When she spotted me, her face broke into a smile.

I ordered a mocha and a croissant, paid, and then carried my tray to her table. "Where is everyone?" I asked as I sat down across from her.

She frowned. "I don't think anyone else is coming."

She fingered a stack of file folders in front of her that I guessed were for stories. I broke off a piece of the croissant and ate it.

"Did you write anything?" she asked.

I shook my head. "I tried, Melissa. I really did. I started something on salmon. But what I wrote sounded like an eighth-grade report. A bad one."

She looked away. "It doesn't matter. Thomas is the only one who submitted anything, and all his stuff is sports. Annie hasn't written a word—I'm sure that's why she's not here. Natasha spends all her time studying for the SAT. I'll never get an issue out before Christmas. Mr. Bresnan is my faculty advisor, and he doesn't care. He gets paid the same if there's one newspaper or if there's ten. I thought if it was a great newspaper it might help me get into Stanford, but the whole thing is going to be a total failure."

"You'll get in anyway. You've got good grades."

She managed a weak smile. "You need more than good grades for Stanford. You have to show something special for them. And there's nothing special about me."

"That's not true," I said, and right away I felt stupid.

She reached over and put her hand on mine. "That's sweet, Chance."

After that we sipped our drinks and talked about Arnold's class. I was in no hurry to finish, and she wasn't either. Finally, around ten, she stretched. "It's so warm in here, I'm getting sleepy. Do you want to go for a walk? Sunset Hill Park isn't too far."

We took Thirty-fourth Avenue, a quiet, dark street on the bluff above the marina. The night was clear and cold, with more stars in the sky than usual. When we reached the park, she stopped, leaned against the chainlink fence, and pointed down to the marina. "Can you see your boat?" she said.

"I can pick out the pier," I said. "But that's it. Our boat is small."

A barge, probably carrying sand headed for Salmon Bay Gravel, was gliding across Puget Sound. A couple of big freighters were anchored offshore.

"Those ships are ugly when you see them up close," she said, "yet they're beautiful at night from a distance."

A chill wind came up, and she leaned into me for warmth. I put my arm around her, and she leaned in closer. For a long time, neither of us said anything. Finally, a foghorn broke the silence. "I've got to get home," she said, looking at her watch.

For the first few blocks walking back, it was as if we were alone in the world. That she was headed for Stanford and I was headed nowhere didn't seem to matter. But when we reached streets with more traffic, we pulled apart. By the time we'd reached her car, the mood that had brought us together was gone.

"I've been thinking about the newspaper," she said.

"What about it?"

"Natasha's idea was good. I talked to my dad. He says he doesn't think there's much danger from terrorists, but that there always is smuggling on a waterfront. He says that if you kept your eyes open, you might see something. Now that would really make a great story."

I tried to keep my voice level. "Melissa, if the cops can't find smugglers, how can I?"

"It's just an idea," she said. "It can't hurt to keep your eyes open."

CHAPTER TWELVE

It was early Saturday morning, not even eight o'clock. The sky was wet and gray. I was headed to Little Coney for breakfast. That was something I'd started doing every Saturday now that I had a little money. As I walked along the marina, I pulled my coat tightly around me and buried my hands in my pockets.

I stopped at the newspaper rack in front of Pier M to buy a newspaper for my dad. I stuck a quarter into the slot and opened the rack. The top newspaper was wrinkled, so I took one from further down in the stack. "Two Soldiers Killed" the headline shouted. I read the first sentence of the article and folded the newspaper in half. When I turned around, the fat guy was standing behind me. "Come with me," he said.

I followed him into the marina office. On Saturday, the office didn't open until nine, so we were the only ones there. When we stepped inside, he turned on the light, but he kept the blinds down. I followed him to his desk in the back. I sat down in a blue plastic chair as he slid into his swivel chair.

"Is there someplace on the boat where you could store things for a little while?" he asked.

"I don't know. I don't think so. Everything's pretty tight already."

"Come on, there has to be someplace. It's worth another hundred dollars a month to you."

I remembered the secret storage nook where Dad kept his service medals and his American flag. It was behind a false panel in my sleeping berth. Unless you knew it was there, you'd never find it. That spot was almost a taboo place—my dad never looked in there. "I guess I could store some packages. Not too many. But what's wrong with what's been going on so far?"

"Nothing's wrong with it. And you're going to keep doing it. Only every once in a while there's going to be a different kind of package. When that happens, you bring it to the boat and store it. You understand?"

"How will I know?"

"You'll know. These packages will look and feel different."

"For how long will I store them?"

"Not long. Somebody will contact you, and then they'll take them off your hands."

"How will they contact me?"

"I don't know and I don't care. But they will."

I stared at him for a long time, searching his dark eyes. Suddenly everything clicked. "That envelope a while back," I said. "That was a trial run, wasn't it? You've got a new customer. Which means you're making double what you made before. So I should get double."

He glared at me. "Double?" he replied contemptuously. "You're not doing anything more than what you've been doing. You're lucky to be getting an extra hundred bucks. Don't push it, kid."

I didn't back down. "I want double," I said. Then I leaned forward. "I could go to the police, you know. I could tell them all about you."

The fat guy jumped to his feet, reached across his desk, grabbed me by the shirt, and yanked me out of the chair with a strength I wouldn't have thought he had. His eyes darkened chillingly. "Listen and listen good. This isn't some high school poker game you're involved with. If the wrong people heard you talk about the police, we could both end up in body bags. Understand?" He jerked me forward so that my face was inches from his. "Understand!"

"I understand," I whispered, my throat so tight I could hardly speak.

Still he kept squeezing, and fear roared through my body. "Say it again. Only this time I want to hear it."

"I understand," I said, my voice louder. He shoved me back into my plastic chair. I slumped down, my heart racing.

"You think I'm scary, kid? I'm Mother Teresa, that's who I am, compared to the other people involved in this. Now get out of here."

I stood, my knees like Jell-O, and made my way to the door. I opened it, stepped outside, and walked about halfway back to the boat. Then I stopped and leaned over the railing and vomited.

I was out of my league. The people I was dealing with were criminals. Big-time criminals. Million-dollar criminals. I didn't see them, but that didn't mean they didn't see me. I had to be very careful. And as soon as I could, I had to get out.

CHAPTER THIRTEEN

Over Christmas break, my dad would get up early every morning, shave, and leave before I even got out of my bed. He never said where he was going, and I never asked. Maybe he was going to Labor Ready, a place for men to get temporary jobs, or maybe he was drinking at the Sloop Tavern. Probably one day it was one place, and the next it was the other.

I slept for as long as I possibly could those mornings. Then I'd get up and hang out around the marina and along Market Street. On decent days, I'd walk to Great Harvest bakery. They give away big hunks of warm bread as samples. I'd get a piece, then sit down at one of the tables and—surrounded by the smell of baking bread and the warmth of the ovens—eat it as slowly as I possibly could. A couple of times I caught matinees at the Majestic Bay. Still, the days dragged.

On Christmas Eve, my dad found some hemlock branches

that had been downed by a windstorm. He stuck them in a bucket filled with sand and stood them up in the corner of the cabin. "What do you think of our Christmas tree?" he said.

"It's great," I said, but I wished he'd done nothing.

Christmas morning I gave him a book on the exploration of Antarctica that I'd bought at Secret Garden bookstore. He read the title and then flipped the book over. "This is about Roald Amundsen." He skimmed the first paragraph, and then looked up. "Amundsen was a great man, Chance. A great explorer. Thank you very much."

He shoved a plastic bag toward me. I opened it; inside were gloves made of some high-tech fabric. "I got them at a bike shop," he said. "They're supposed to keep you warm but not make you sweaty."

"They're great, Dad," I said. "Thanks."

"I figured sometimes your hands must get cold when you run."

"They do. These will be great."

"All right, then. Not such a bad Christmas after all."

I ran at my regular time that afternoon, and then I went to the movies. I thought the theater would be empty, but it was nearly full. The movie was some comedy whose name I can't remember. Around me, people laughed like crazy. When the movie ended, I walked back to the marina. I thought I'd have the boat to myself, but my dad was waiting for me down in the cabin. "Let's go to dinner," he said.

We went to Charley's, a restaurant on the waterfront not too far from our pier. When the waiter came around, I ordered a hamburger. My dad shook his head. "You're getting a New York steak," he said. "And I'm getting the same."

"Anything to drink?" the waiter asked.

"Coke," I said.

"The same for me," my dad said, which surprised me.

I guess I must have looked nervous about the money he was spending, because he told me to stop worrying. "I've been working steady all week at Ballard Bicycles. Assembling bikes, that sort of thing."

After that we sat at the table, neither of us talking. Finally the food came. I'd been eating canned and packaged meals for so long that I'd forgotten how good a steak dinner at a restaurant could be. The meat was pink and juicy; the mashed potatoes buttery; the carrots glazed in brown sugar. After he took his first bite of the steak, my dad looked up. "Good, isn't it?"

"Yeah," I said, "it is."

When we had both finished eating, he put the napkin down by his plate and looked at me. "There's a chance they'll keep me on at the bike shop. If they do, I want you to quit that job of yours. You understand?"

"Sure, Dad," I said.

He leaned forward. "I mean it, Chance. If they hire full-time, I want you to quit that job. I don't like anything about it."

"You don't know anything about it," I said.

"I know you get paid in cash, Chance. You try to hide that wad of bills, but I've seen it. Delivering stuff on the waterfront for cash—I wasn't born yesterday."

I looked out the window. "Say I quit and then you lose your job. Where will we be then?"

"I won't lose it, Chance."

The family at the table across from us all broke into laughter over something. We both looked over; the man was laughing so hard tears came to his eyes.

"OK," I said. "If they hire you full-time, I'll quit."

CHAPTER FOURTEEN

When I'd first started working for the fat guy, I figured the lousy weather in the winter would empty the beach and make it easier for me to search through the rocks for packages without worrying that someone would see me and get suspicious. But it was almost January, and every day people were still out combing the beach.

These weren't muscle builders or babes working on their suntans. They were winter beach people, and they were looking for things: herons and eagles, starfish and sea pens. They held binoculars to their eyes, and they knew the beach like I knew the *Tiny Dancer*. They made me nervous, so I took to running as close to nightfall as I dared. It was harder to see if I ran late, but the later I ran, the more deserted the beach was.

New Year's Day I waited until it was so dark that I almost didn't find the package. I spotted it just as I was turning to head back. The wrapping was different from the other packages; the paper was reddish and coarse. And whatever was inside felt different too, though I immediately knew I'd felt something like it before. Finally it came to me—it had the consistency of Play-Doh.

This was the new stuff.

I slipped the package into my backpack and headed back to the marina. But instead of bringing the package to the locker, I kept it on the *Tiny Dancer*. My dad was working at the bike shop, so it was simple to go below deck, climb into my berth, slide open the panel to the secret storage nook, lift out his medals and his perfectly folded American flag, and hide the package behind them.

I'd gotten used to sleeping late, so it was hard getting out of bed the Monday winter break ended. As I dragged myself up the hill toward Lincoln High, the skies opened and a freezing rain poured down. I walked fast, but still I was drenched by the time I made it to school. As I pushed open the main doors, I spotted a stack of school newspapers by the front door.

I grabbed a copy and headed to the commons area, hoping it would be warm in there. Other kids must have had the same idea; it was so crowded I had to sit on the floor.

For the ten minutes before my first class, I skimmed through Thomas Dowell's articles on the football team, the girls' volleyball team, and the soccer team. Annie Comstock wrote something on the ecology club; Natasha Martin had a description of the new biotech academy. Melissa wrote everything else. Some junior had come in third at a chess competition; four kids were National Merit Scholarship semifinalists;

one of the football players worked with Habitat for Humanity. She wrote other stuff, too, stuff that I didn't read.

Almost everybody in the commons was flipping through the newspaper. But when the bell rang, most kids left it behind on the tables or tossed it in the trash.

I didn't see Melissa until just before sixth period. "It's a good newspaper," I said, holding up my copy. "Really good."

"Thanks," she said, her smile forced. "The next one will be better."

That night my dad and I ate dinner together, something we'd been doing more and more of. Afterwards, I could see him getting edgy. "There's a Sonics game on television later. You want to watch it?"

"Yeah," he said. "Let's do that."

It was a decent game, but around eight the wind started blowing and the boat started rocking. The reception was affected, and the picture flickered. Finally my dad switched off the television.

"I find out tomorrow," he said. "About the job at the cycle shop. The guy I work for is just the manager. He has to ask the owner if he can keep me on. I have a good feeling about this, Chance. I'm due for a little luck." He stood and stretched. "I'm going to go for a walk."

Something in my face must have betrayed my thoughts.

"Don't worry. I'm just going for a walk."

CHAPTER FIFTEEN

On the blackboard in Arnold's class the next day were two words: Yellow Alert. "How many of you knew the terrorism alert status today is yellow? Anyone?" Kids looked around at one another and smiled nervously. "How many of you knew we had a color-coded terrorism alert system?" A few hands went up.

"I know it exists," Brian Mitchell said. "But I don't pay attention to it. We're out here in Seattle. Why would al-Qaida terrorists attack us? Nothing ever happens in the Northwest."

"You sound disappointed," said a new kid.

"I'm glad nothing ever happens here," Heather said. "I don't want anything bad to happen."

"What about Ressam?" Arnold said.

"Who's Ressam?" Melody Turner asked.

Arnold told the story. This guy Ahmed Ressam had tried to

sneak into Port Angeles on a ferry from Canada right around the New Year in 2000. When he was arrested, the police found explosives in the trunk of his car. At first, they thought he was trying to blow up the Space Needle, but it turned out he was headed to Los Angeles to blow up the airport there.

I'd never heard about him, and I don't think anybody else in class had either—though a couple of kids pretended they had. Port Angeles is a sleepy little town on the Olympic Peninsula. A totally nowhere place. It was weird to think that some international terrorist had been caught there.

For the rest of class, kids talked about terrorists and Iraq and Afghanistan. I looked out the window and thought about my dad. He'd probably know about the job by now. They wouldn't make him wait until the end of the day.

When school ended, I walked back to the boat. As I came down the pier, I saw my dad on deck, sitting at the little table smoking a cigarette and drinking from a coffee cup.

"They're not ready to hire me just yet," he said as soon as I stepped on the boat. "It doesn't mean that they won't hire me later, though. This just isn't a busy time for bike shops. In the spring they're almost sure they'll call me back."

"That makes sense," I said. "You've got to keep yourself ready, Dad. For when they call."

He held up his cup. "There's just coffee in here, Chance. Nothing else. I'm trying."

I changed into my running stuff and ran my normal route. There was no package. After I'd showered, I headed back to the boat. The weather had turned windy—a storm was coming.

My dad was below deck, and I joined him. I stuck some frozen lasagna in the oven for dinner, and we somehow managed to eat it even though the boat was heaving back and forth.

As the evening wore on, the winds increased and so did the rocking. It was impossible to read or watch television. I finally climbed into my berth, pulled the blankets up around my neck, and tried to listen to the radio. Outside, pulleys were clanking against the masts of sailboats, making a racket.

My dad, who'd been at the table flipping through the newspaper and smoking, stood and stretched. "I think I'll go to Little Coney. Get something hot to drink and get off this damn boat."

"Sounds good. You mind if I come with you?"

"Of course not. I'd like the company. But I wasn't going drinking, if that's what you were worried about."

I was afraid Little Coney might be closed, but it wasn't. I ordered a hot chocolate; my dad got a large coffee. "Take your time," the guy behind the counter said as he slid the cups to us. "My daughter has my car and she won't be here for another hour, easy."

We took a booth in the corner. A Beatles song, "Here Comes the Sun," was playing through the speakers. "Not likely," my dad said.

"What?"

"The sun. Not too likely to come." He poured four packets of sugar into his coffee, stirred it up, and took a sip. "Terrible, but hot," he whispered. "How's the chocolate?"

"The same."

I looked out the window toward Puget Sound. The wind had whipped up whitecaps; big clouds were racing across the moonlit sky. It felt great to be warm and snug when outside everything was cold and wild.

"Anything interesting happen at school?" my dad said. It was an ordinary question, but it had been years since he'd asked it.

"Not really," I said. "We talked about terrorism. Red Alert and Yellow Alert and stuff like that. I didn't even know we had codes."

He shook his head. "That color stuff is a load of crap. Nobody pays any attention to it."

"That's what my teacher said. But he says we should pay attention because Seattle is a target." I paused. "What would be worth blowing up around here?"

My dad rubbed the back of his neck. "The Space Needle is what everybody says, and that's probably what terrorists would hit. But if I were a terrorist, I'd blow up the Ballard Locks."

"The locks?" I said. "Who would care if the locks were gone?"

"This whole region would care, that's who. Blow up the locks, and Lake Washington and Lake Union would drain right out into Puget Sound. A big stinking mud hole is all that would be left. It would be a disaster for the shipping industry and for tourism. Pick the right day—the opening of boating season, for example—and you'd kill a lot of people too. Or you could blow up the I-5 Bridge, or attack one of those big cruise ships, or blow up a ferry. Puget Sound is full of soft targets."

"Do you think anything like that will ever really happen?"

He pushed his cup away from him. "Not really, but you

never know. I mean, who would have ever thought that September eleventh would happen?"

He stayed sober for a week. But when I came home from school the following Thursday, he had a bottle of beer in his hand. Friday afternoon he wasn't on the boat at all.

CHAPTER SIXTEEN

It was a cold January day. I was running out to the tree, wearing the gloves my dad had bought me for Christmas, when I spotted someone poking around in the rocks, their back to me. Immediately I started racing forward as fast as I could, my heart pounding. I didn't know what I was going to do, but I knew I had to do something. As I came closer, I recognized the brown hair and the strong, straight shoulders.

It was Melissa.

"What are you doing here?" I shouted.

She smiled when she first saw me, but the anger in my voice chased the smile away. "I was looking for the rat's nest," she said.

"You've got no business being here, Melissa."

Now anger came into her eyes. "It's a public beach, Chance. You don't own it."

I looked around. Was the fat guy watching us?

"I know I don't own it," I said, trying to soften my tone.

She looked at me, and then up the beach. "Who are you looking for?"

"No one."

"Well, if you're not looking for anyone, then why do you keep turning around? And just where are these famous rats, anyway?"

"They're in there," I said. "You just don't know where to look."

"Show me."

"No. You'd disturb them and then they might kill their babies or bite you or something."

She eyed me suspiciously. "And you don't disturb them when you look?" She paused. "You're just making this up, aren't you? There are no rats. What is this all about, Chance?"

"I'm not making anything up," I said, trying to sound calm. "There is a rat's nest in there."

"So why won't you show it to me?"

"Melissa, would you please go? As a favor to me."

"And what if I don't go? What then?"

"Please, Melissa. Don't do this. You're going to screw everything up for me."

"Screw what up?"

"Would you please just go?"

She looked at me for what seemed like forever, and then turned away from the rocks. "All right. I'll go. But something is going on, and I'm going to find out what it is."

"Nothing is—"

"Stop lying to me, Chance," she said. Then she turned and headed toward the trail that led through upper Golden Gardens Park to her house. I watched until she was swallowed up by the trees. Only then did I return to the marina.

The next afternoon the fat guy was waiting for me by the ramp as I returned from school. "Let's walk," he said, and I followed him toward Pier A, where the huge yachts were moored. Once we were hidden from the road by the dry-dock area, he stopped. "Who was the girl?"

"What girl?" I said.

"Don't play games, kid."

I took a deep breath. "She's just a girl from school."

"What's her name?"

I started to tell him, then held back. "Alice something. I don't know her very well. She's just a girl from school."

His eyes flashed dangerously. "What was she doing on the beach?"

"Nothing. She lives up on the bluff. There's a path that comes down."

"And she just happened to be there as you arrived? A total coincidence."

"Maybe she likes me a little. What can I do?"

"A romance. How touching. What can you do?" His tone had been mock-sweet, but now it changed. "You can make her not like you, that's what you can do. Because if you do like her, then you want her clear of this. For her sake, and for yours, and for mine. Understand?"

I nodded.

"Good. Now make it happen."

The fat guy was right. One hundred percent right. I was taking risks, but I knew what they were and I knew why I was taking them. Melissa was walking into this thing blind. I had to get her off my track. But how?

CHAPTER SEVENTEEN

That Friday night I sat in the *Tiny Dancer's* cabin, thinking. Maybe Melissa would be at the Blue Note Café for her newspaper staff meeting. If I showed up, maybe I'd be able to talk to her alone. That was a lot of *maybes,* but I had to take the chance.

A cold mist—almost a fog—chilled the air, and me. It was so cold that for once I didn't mind climbing the stairway that led from the marina to the café because the climb warmed me. At the top I caught my breath, then crossed the street and stepped inside the café and looked around.

Melissa, her shoulders slumped forward, was sitting alone at a small table in the back corner. No Thomas Dowell, no Natasha Martin, no nobody. I thought she would still be angry with me, but when our eyes met, she smiled.

I ordered a mocha and a blueberry muffin. After I paid I walked over to her table. "OK if I sit here?"

"I want you to. I'm feeling a little lonely, to be honest."

"Where is everybody?"

She shrugged. "How would I know? I guess the success of our first issue drove them all away."

"It was a good newspaper," I said.

"That's nice of you to say, but it isn't true."

Steam rose from the muffin as I pulled it apart. "Do you want some?" I asked.

She shook her head. I took a bite, then another. Melissa fidgeted with her spoon.

I sipped the mocha and then fingered the muffin liner. "I'm sorry about the way I acted on the beach," I said. "I didn't mean to be mean."

"Chance, what was that all about? And don't lie to me. Please."

I looked away for a moment, and then I looked back. "As soon as I can, I'll explain everything to you. Absolutely everything. But until then you've got to promise me that you'll stay off the beach and away from the marina."

Her eyes clouded. "Are you in trouble, Chance?"

"No," I said. "I'm not in trouble."

"You're lying. I can tell."

I looked back at her. "I'm not in trouble, Melissa. But if you keep poking around on the beach, you'll get me in trouble. And you'll get yourself in trouble, too."

Her eyes locked on mine. "How long until you tell me?"

"I don't know for sure. June, at the latest. Maybe sooner."

"And you'll tell me absolutely everything?"

"I told you I would."

"Promise me."

I made a cross on my chest with the index finger of my right hand. "Hope to die."

She smiled, but after that, neither of us talked for a while.

"You want something else?" I said when she finished her espresso.

"No thanks. I know it's cold, but I wouldn't mind walking a bit, like we did before."

I wanted to say yes. I wanted to walk with her and slide my arm around her. But when you're bobbing around in the ocean, when you're barely keeping your own head above the water, you can't reach out to anybody, because if you do grab hold, you might pull them under with you. "I can't, Melissa," I said.

"Why not?"

"I just can't."

"And you won't be coming on Friday nights anymore, will you?"

"No, I won't."

"OK then," she said, and she stood up and stuck out her hand.

I shook it. "OK then," I said.

PART THREE

CHAPTER ONE

All through February and March, things went the way the fat guy wanted them to go. Melissa stayed away from the rocks on the beach and stayed away from me at school, so I didn't worry that I was leading her into danger. I picked up the regular packages and brought them to the locker room in the regular way. The red packages, which came almost every Saturday morning, still spooked me. I didn't like the squishiness of them, or the way the coarse paper felt, and I definitely didn't like storing them on the *Tiny Dancer*. But I did like the money. The money paid the moorage fee and the electric bill. The icebox was stocked with food, and so were the shelves above it and below it.

I suppose I should have been happy, or at least less unhappy, but it didn't work that way. From the first day the fat man talked to me, I knew I was being used by people who didn't care what happened to me. In the beginning, it had all been exciting too, exciting like riding a roller coaster is exciting. Only when you're on a roller coaster, you know that in a minute you're going to get off and the world will return to normal. I hadn't gotten off; nothing was ever normal for me. Every time I saw a cop car in the marina parking lot or heard a siren in the distance, I thought the police were coming after me.

Twice I ran into Jeff Creager. Both times he made a point of asking about my job. "It's great," I said both times. "A lot better than washing dishes. A lot better." He laughed and wished me luck, but once he was gone a sick feeling would come over me, because I knew it wasn't better. It wasn't better at all.

We might have been able to make it, my dad and me, if I'd stayed at Ray's. When he lost his job, I thought the only money we'd have would be the money I earned. But it hadn't turned out that way. People on the marina know one another. Once the word got out that my dad needed work, men had hired him to help scrape or paint or clean their boats. It wasn't steady work, but it was work. By pooling the money he made doing those odd jobs with my paycheck from Ray's, we might have had enough— especially if we had hit up the food bank more often.

Sometimes when I was running, I'd think about how things might have turned out if I'd kept washing dishes. Instead of chasing Melissa away, I'd have been able to hang out with her. I could have eaten lunch with her at school, talked with her at the Blue Note on Friday nights, maybe even done other stuff with her. Then I'd give myself a shake. Who was I kidding? If I were still working at Ray's, I'd have no extra money in my pocket to do anything with anybody. Besides, Melissa lived in a different world; there was no way I was ever getting in.

CHAPTER TWO

The first Monday in April was cold and rainy. The boat rocked so much on Sunday night I hardly slept. There aren't many Mondays when I'm eager to go to school, but that was one. I wanted off that boat.

On Mondays the hallways at Lincoln are always loud. Kids are talking about their weekends—the sports they played, the dates they had, the beer they drank. But when I stepped inside Lincoln that morning, I knew something was wrong. It was too quiet, and too many kids were clumped together, their faces glum.

Melissa was in a corner with Annie and Natasha. We hadn't talked much since that night at the Blue Note, but as soon as she saw me, she came over. "Have you heard?" she asked, her voice shaky as if she were about to cry.

"Heard what?"

"About Brent Miller."

"What about Brent Miller?"

"He's dead."

I stared at her. "He's dead. How?"

"He was on patrol in Iraq. There was some sort of bomb on a bridge and two soldiers died. He was one of them."

"Are you sure?"

She nodded. "It was on the radio this morning."

"The news gets stuff wrong all the time. You know that."

"Chance, he's dead."

The first bell sounded. "I've got to go," Melissa said. "I've got a calculus test, though I don't know how I'm going to do any calculus today."

All day I kept hoping to see Melissa so I could talk to her some more, but I didn't see her again until Arnold's class. Even then she came late, so I had no chance to speak with her before class.

Arnold looked old as he stood in front of us. The room was totally quiet as he pulled down the map of the world. "I know you've all heard the news about Brent Miller," he said, his voice weary. "I don't know much, but I'll tell you the little I do know. It happened outside of Baghdad. Brent was assigned to . . ."

As Arnold talked I tried to listen, but my mind kept drifting back to September. I saw Miller standing in front of the class again. I remembered the way he'd acted, both that day and before. I hadn't liked him, and I didn't feel bad about not liking him. But I didn't want him to be dead. I didn't want anybody to be dead.

I looked to Arnold. "You hear that one soldier was killed here, or two there," he was saying, "and it doesn't make much of an impact. But each one of those soldiers has a family, has friends, has a story, just like Brent did. Each one of them had a life they never got to lead."

When class ended, we all filed out silently. But as soon as we were in the hall, Brian Mitchell confronted Melissa. "I bet you're happy," he hissed. "'The dumb soldier got what he deserved.' That's what you're thinking. You should join al-Qaida if you hate America so much. Go bow down to Allah. You make me sick."

Melissa's face went white and she burst into tears. I stepped between Brian and her. "Shut up, Mitchell," I said.

He wheeled around. "Don't tell me to shut up. I'll say whatever I want to say. You're as bad as she is, anyway."

A crowd had formed around us. "You're being a moron, Brian," I said.

That's when he started throwing punches. I should have been expecting it, but I didn't get my hands up until he'd smacked me once right in the face. I grabbed him around the waist and wrestled him to the ground. We thrashed around trying to punch each other for a minute or so. Then somebody grabbed me from behind, and I guess somebody must have grabbed him too. A minute later I heard Arnold's voice. "What's going on here?"

"Nothing," I said, twisting free from whoever was holding me.

"What do you mean, nothing?"

"I mean nothing."

"So why's your nose bleeding?"

I put my hand to my face and felt the hot blood. "It's nothing," I repeated.

"It's not nothing," Arnold said. He looked to Brian Mitchell. "Both of you come with me."

Once we reached the main office, Arnold went to find the nurse, Ms. Tolbert. She handed me a small towel and had me lean forward and pinch my nose. "Don't lean your head back or you'll swallow your own blood."

I was still pinching my nose when Ms. Dugan appeared in the doorway. "Come with me," she said.

I followed her to her office. Brian Mitchell was slouched in a chair by the window, his arms folded across his chest. Dugan motioned for me to sit in the chair next to him.

"You fight, you get suspended. It's that simple. We have a zero-tolerance policy, and you both know it." She picked up the telephone. "I'm calling your folks, Chance. What's your phone number?"

I looked at the floor.

"Come on. What's your number? I can get it from the secretary, you know."

"I don't have a phone number," I said.

"What do you mean, you don't have a phone number?"

"Just what I said."

"How about a cell phone?"

I shook my head.

"Your mom or dad got a work number?"

Again I shook my head.

"So how does a person get in touch with them?"

"Ms. Dugan, I'm pretty much on my own. So if there's something you want to say, just say it to me."

Brian cleared his throat. "How about if Chance and me just shake hands and go home." Brian turned to look at me. "You'll shake my hand, won't you?"

"Sure," I said. "I'll shake your hand." He stuck his hand out and I shook it.

"OK?" Mitchell said, looking to Dugan.

Dugan stared at me, and then at Mitchell. "All right. I'll ignore what happened. But this ends here. You understand? You two don't even bump shoulders in the hall or I will suspend you."

I nodded. So did Brian.

Dugan motioned with her right hand. "Go on, get out of here. Brent Miller has us all frazzled."

Mitchell and I walked down the long empty hall side by side. I tried to think of something to say, but nothing came to me. When he reached the main doors, he pushed them open and took the stairs two at a time. I watched him until he had crossed the street. Then I started down the stairs myself.

Melissa was sitting on the bottom stair waiting for me. When she saw me, she stood and faced me. "Did you get suspended?" she asked.

I shook my head.

"That's good." She paused. "Thanks for coming to my defense. Again."

I shrugged. "He was out of line."

She looked down; her voice was quiet. "Do you think other kids think the way he does? That I'm glad Brent Miller died?"

"Nobody thinks that, Melissa. Mitchell doesn't even think that. He was just being an idiot."

She raised her head. "I didn't like him, but I didn't want him to die."

"Everybody knows that, Melissa." Her green eyes were all watery; looking at her made my throat tighten. "Nobody wanted anything bad to happen to him."

I looked at my watch. I needed to get back to the marina to run. "I've got to get going," I said.

She nodded. "I do too. But come to the Blue Note on Friday. OK? I have to talk to you about something."

I shook my head. "No, Melissa. There's no point."

"I told the others that there wasn't going to be a meeting. I have to talk to you, Chance. I have to."

"Whatever it is, just say it now, Melissa."

She shook her head. "There's something I have to show you." She paused. "The Blue Note, Friday. Is that so hard?"

"All right," I said. "Friday."

CHAPTER THREE

A person dies, a person you know, and you should think about them. All week I tried to think about Brent Miller. But my mind kept going back to Melissa—what did she want to say to me? What did she want to show me?

Then on Thursday afternoon, my dad called out to me from down below the moment I stepped on the boat. "That you, Chance?"

"Yeah," I said. "It's me."

He came topside. "Sit down," he said.

"I was going to go running now."

"Sit down, Chance. This won't take long."

I sat down, and he sat across from me. The boat rocked back and forth. I tried to act calm, but inside I was in knots. First Melissa, then my dad. Were things coming apart all around me, and was I the only one who didn't know it?

Finally he spoke. "This morning the port police went up

and down every single pier in the marina. They had their dogs with them."

"Oh yeah," I said, trying to act unconcerned.

"Yeah," he said. "They asked me if they could board."

My heart was pounding so loudly I was afraid he'd hear it. "What did you say?"

"I told them that this was America and that they could go to hell. So did most of the owners on the pier."

"What did they do then?"

"They laughed, but they wrote down the name of our sail-boat."

"Do you think they'll come back?"

"No. If they were coming back, they'd have been here hours ago." He tilted his head back and took a long drink of the beer he was holding, finishing it off. "Would it matter?" he asked.

"Would what matter?"

"If they came back."

"Not to me," I said. "I've got nothing to hide."

He stared at me, and I forced myself not to look away.

"Well, neither do I. So we've got nothing to worry about, do we?"

CHAPTER FOUR

I was ten minutes early when I stepped into the Blue Note that Friday night, but Melissa was already sitting at a table in the back corner. She was reading the newspaper, and her face looked older, more grown-up. I wondered if I looked older too.

I went to the counter and ordered a mocha and coffee cake. When my order was ready, I carried my plate and cup to her table and sat across from her. She didn't greet me with either a word or a smile. I took a sip of my drink and a bite of my cake. "OK," I said, trying to keep my voice light. "I'm here. What's this all about?"

"I figured it out, Chance."

"Figured what out?"

"Don't play dumb. You're involved in a smuggling ring, aren't you?"

I chewed the cake, swallowed, and then took a sip of the mocha.

"Well, aren't you?" she repeated.

"I don't know what you're talking about," I said.

"I'm talking about the packages you pick up on the beach. They're filled with drugs, aren't they?"

Beads of sweat broke out on my forehead. "I told you—I don't know what you're talking about."

"Stop lying, Chance."

The net seemed to be closing around me. First the police on the pier, now Melissa. I'd thought I was being so clever, fooling everyone, and it turned out I was fooling no one. I was tired of the lying, tired of the hiding, tired of the constant fear.

"I don't really know what's in the packages, Melissa," I said quietly. "I don't know where they come from or where they end up. I just pick them up, take them to a locker, and leave them there. That's all I do."

"Don't be stupid. It's drugs. What else could it be?" Her tone was contemptuous.

"You're probably right. All I'm saying is that I've never looked inside any of them. I just pick them up, Melissa. I don't even know how they get on the beach."

"Do you want to know? Because I can tell you."

I thought for a moment. Did I want to know? The fat guy had said knowing was dangerous. But not knowing had its risk too.

"Yeah," I said. "I do."

She reached down and pulled out a stack of photographs from her backpack. Then she moved her chair so we were sitting side by side. "Do you know a boat named *Bob's Toy*?" she asked.

Everybody on the marina knew *Bob's Toy*. It was one of those million-dollar yachts wealthy people charter to go on whale-watching trips to the San Juan Islands and other places like that. "Sure, I know it," I said. "It's for rich people who want to see the sights without dealing with the crowds on the big cruise ships."

"They do more than show rich people the sights," she said. She showed me a picture of *Bob's Toy* sailing into Puget Sound. As she talked, she flipped from one photo to the next. "When the yacht gets to within half a mile of Shilshole marina, two kayakers drop into the water. The tourists come up on deck to watch and take photos as the kayakers race to the shore. Maybe they bet on which kayak will get there first. Or maybe they're told it's some sort of Native American tradition. It doesn't really matter. What matters is that the kayakers hit the beach right where your rat's nest with all the cute baby rats is supposed to be." She stopped and looked at me. "Were there ever any baby rats?"

"No."

"I figured as much," she said, flipping to the next photo. "The two kayakers pull the kayaks onto the shore. They wave to the tourists on the boat, have a drink of water or something, and then slip a package out of the kayak and into the rocks. It's very clever, don't you think? They do their smuggling in front of everybody. They call attention to themselves, so no one suspects they're doing anything wrong." She had one more picture, which was face-down on the table.

"What's that one?" I asked.

"This one?" she said. "This is the one that could put you in prison." She turned it over. It was a photo of me pulling a package out of the rocks.

I swallowed. "I thought we had an agreement. I told you I'd tell you everything as soon as I could, but instead of waiting, you've been spying on me."

She shook her head. "That's not fair, Chance. I promised you I wouldn't go back down to the beach. And I haven't. But that's all I promised. Do you think the newspaper stuff is a joke to me? Because it isn't. I want to be a top-notch reporter someday. Reporters investigate. You acted guilty that day on the beach. You acted guilty the last time we met here. So I decided to find out the truth, and I did."

As she spoke, she gathered up all the photos and put them back in the file folder. She shoved the folder into her backpack, zipped it shut, and then looked at me. "There's one thing I don't get."

"What?" I said, glowering at her.

"It's my guess that drugs or alcohol or both have ruined your father's life. Am I right?"

"My father has ruined his own life. Every bum on the street ruins his own life."

"But why be part of it, Chance? You see what it does to people. More than anybody, you should want to stay clear. Is the money that important to you? What do you need it for, anyway?"

There it was, right there in her question. The difference between her and me. She knew things I didn't. Lots of things.

But it went both ways, because I knew all about a world she couldn't even imagine.

"What do I need it for?" I said. "I need it for the moorage fee, for food, for clothes, for heat and electricity, for sewage. I need it for my toothpaste and soap and my dad's booze and his cigarettes. I need it so that I can sit here with you and have a mocha and eat a piece of coffee cake. That's what I need it for."

She looked at me in disbelief. "You pay all the bills?"

"Yeah. I do."

She sat back in her chair and stared at me. "I didn't know."

"Now you do," I said.

Melissa didn't say anything for a long time. The door to the café opened a few times, a gust of cold wind entering as people came and went. Finally she glanced at the clock on the wall. "I can't stay. My aunt Catherine is visiting from New Jersey and I promised I'd be home by nine." She gathered her stuff together and then looked at me. "You didn't have to do it," she said, her voice low. "My father would have helped. All you had to do was ask and he would have helped. He still would."

"I'm not a beggar, Melissa, and neither is my dad."

"Sooner or later you're going to get caught. You know that, don't you?"

CHAPTER FIVE

After she left, I sat looking at my half-eaten cake. Then an idea came to me. I went to the counter and asked the waitress for paper and a pencil. She gave them to me, and I returned to the table. It didn't take long to get the answer. Three weeks. Twenty-one days. That's how long I had to keep running to make enough money to get us through May and June. As soon as I graduated, I'd go to the recruiting office by Northgate and enlist. By July 1, I'd be on my own.

As I stared at the numbers on the paper, I thought about my dad. What was going to happen to him when I was gone? Would he be able to get his act together without me around? I wanted to think he would, but I just didn't know.

I bused my dishes, and then headed down the steep stairway that led to the marina. Once I was under the tree cover, it was so dark I couldn't see my feet in front of me. Overhead the limbs in the treetops were tossing back and forth.

When I came out from under the trees at the bottom of the stairway, I turned and started toward the pier. Then I stopped. It was Friday night. I knew where the regular stuff came from; Melissa had solved that for me. But all I knew about the red packages was that they turned up on Saturday. Melissa had watched the drop spot during the day, but never at night.

I don't know why I cared where they came from. Maybe it was because I was quitting. Maybe I didn't want to quit and not know how it had all worked. Whatever the reason, instead of going to the sailboat, I walked out to the drop spot. I checked around in the rocks and found nothing, so nothing had happened yet. About fifty feet past the maple tree is a small recess in the rocks. I slipped into it. From there I could see back to the tree without being seen. I looked at my watch. One hour. That's how long I'd wait. If I was lucky, something might turn up.

The hour came and went. I was hunkered down out of the wind, but I could hear it in the trees and in the fury with which the waves were attacking the beach. If I were back on the boat, I'd be rolling this way and that, miserable. Might as well stay put, I thought.

It was almost midnight when I heard the train whistle. I looked toward the Edmonds oil refineries and saw the head-light of the train engine work its way south, down the shore-line toward me. A freight train, like any other freight train.

The train whistle blew again as it reached the bend above the maple, and as it did, it slowed and finally came to a stop. Nothing unusual about that, either. Another freight train heading north was probably crossing the bridge by the Ballard

Locks. The railroad never runs two trains across that bridge at once.

But as the southbound train sat, puffing in the darkness, a man scrambled down off the caboose. I watched as he eased himself down the boulders leading to the beach. He descended slowly, and in the dim light I saw why—he was holding something in his right hand. He wasn't on the beach long, no more than thirty seconds, before he was climbing back up the rocks and onto the train. Only now he wasn't carrying anything.

So that was it.

A few minutes later, the train lurched into motion again. I moved out from my hiding place and watched as it gathered speed. The back door to the caboose opened and the man stepped onto the platform. He had a large flashlight in his hand, really more of a spotlight than a flashlight, and it bobbed this way and that way as the train chugged forward. Then, suddenly, the light was right in my eyes. I stood blinded for a split second before I dropped down onto the sand and lay still. I stayed face-down, unmoving, as the light passed over me, until the train rumbled out of sight.

CHAPTER SIX

I walked back to the *Tiny Dancer*. As usual, my dad wasn't around. The wind, growing stronger by the minute, was tossing the boats in the marina around. I went below, crawled into my berth to get warm, and leaned my head against the pillow. The stuff from *Bob's Toy*, the stuff Melissa knew about—it was marijuana. I could tell from the smell and feel of it. I'd known it for a long time, even though I'd pretended I didn't. But the stuff in the red packages, the stuff from the train—what was that? And why would somebody run the risk of smuggling those packages into the country and then let them all sit on the *Tiny Dancer* week after week. It didn't make sense.

I twisted around and slid open the panel to the storage nook. I reached inside, removed my dad's medals, and then took out the closest red package. For what had to be the fiftieth time, I put it up to my nose: no odor. I squeezed it; and once again it reminded me of Play-Doh. I turned it this way and that, held it up to the light, even thought about "accidentally" ripping a corner so I could peek inside. But what chance was there that I'd know what it was even if I could see it? At that moment I heard a heavy *clomp* above me. My dad was back. It was so windy I hadn't heard him walking on the pier. My light was on; the storage nook was wide open; his medals were all out on my mattress. As fast as I could, I stuffed the package back into the storage space. He was climbing down into the cabin just as I slid the false panel shut. His medals were still out, so I shoved them under my blankets.

He looked in at me. "What are you doing up, Chance?" His eyes were bloodshot; his words slurred.

"I couldn't sleep," I said. "The wind."

"It is blowing hard, isn't it?"

"Yeah, it is." I paused. "But I think I'll try again, now. I'm pretty tired."

He rummaged through a drawer and pulled out a package of cigarettes. "You do that," he said. "I'll be calling it a night myself right after I have a last cigarette."

He went back up on deck and had his smoke. I slid the panel open and put his medals back. Then I flicked off my light. Five minutes later he came back down, pulled off his boots, and then sighed loudly as he crawled into his berth.

All night the boat rocked back and forth. Any other night, the storm would have kept me up. But now I knew what I had to do. In the morning I'd go to the marina office, see the fat guy, and tell him that it was over for me, that I was quitting. Three more weeks and I'd be out.

I slept.

CHAPTER SEVEN

It was after eight when I woke up Saturday morning. I dressed quickly, and then walked over to the marina office. When I reached it, the CLOSED sign was still hanging in the window. I looked at my watch: I had to wait forty minutes. I walked up and down the marina, looking at my watch every five minutes. Finally, ten minutes after his office was supposed to open, the fat guy's silver Acura pulled into the parking lot.

He struggled to get out of his car, and as he set his car alarm, I came up behind him. When he turned and saw me, he started, fear on his face. Once he registered that it was me, the fear turned to anger. "Don't ever do that again. You hear me?"

"We need to talk," I said.

"Later. I've got to go to work."

"When?"

"Is this really necessary?"

"Yes."

"OK. Six o'clock." He brushed past me.

"Where?"

"You know the overflow parking lot above Golden Gardens?"

"I know it," I said.

He nodded. "There's a path that leads to an open area above the railroad tracks. I'll meet you there."

The day dragged. At three, when the clouds cleared and the sun came out, I did my daily run. The red package was tucked away in the rocks, just where I'd seen the man from the train put it the night before. I stuffed it into my backpack, jogged back, and shoved it into the storage nook beside all the other packages. I counted them: there were twelve.

I walked back up the ramp and took a long shower, but after I'd dressed, it was still only five o'clock. I decided to kill the last hour by heading back to the beach. Little kids were flying high on the swings in the playground; parents were laying out tablecloths and lighting up barbecues. On the grassy fields just past the picnic area, old guys flew fancy kites. At the Teen Center, a group of kids around my age were sitting with their backs to me, facing Puget Sound. Winter was over.

I kept walking, all the way out to the wetland ponds, where I stopped and looked up at the decks on the bluff above the beach. Melissa was probably sitting out on one of them. I could picture her sipping a Coke while she listened to music and talked with her friends about colleges and careers.

I backtracked to the short tunnel that leads to the overflow parking lot. I paced the lot a couple of times, looking for the trail the fat guy had described. Finally I spotted it. I pushed aside a couple of blackberry bushes and hiked about fifty yards to a clearing near the railroad tracks.

Within a couple of minutes the fat guy came puffing around the bend, his face red. "All right," he said as he came up to me. "You wanted to talk; so talk."

I swallowed. "I'm quitting."

His red face got redder. "What are you talking about? You can't quit."

"Well, I am. This is your notice. Three more weeks and I'm done."

His eyes flared. "Is this because the cops were on the piers? That was routine. They're not on to you."

"I'm not quitting because of the cops. I'm quitting because I want to quit."

"And who am I supposed to get to take your place?"

"I don't know. You'll find somebody. You found me, didn't you?"

Some of the anger left his face. He looked up the railroad tracks toward Edmonds. "You're stupid to throw away the money, you know. For as long as you live you'll never make so much for doing so little."

"OK, I'm stupid."

He turned and started toward the parking lot.

"What about the packages on the boat," I said. "What do I do with them?"

"What packages?"

"The red ones. The ones I've been storing."

His eyes widened. "You still have those?"

"Yeah," I said.

"How many of them?"

"I've got all of them."

"How many is all?"

"Twelve. I counted them today."

"Christ, that's sixty pounds minimum. Maybe one hundred pounds."

"What's in them?"

"And they're all on your boat?"

I nodded. "Yeah. Now will you tell me what's in them?"

He shook his head. "I told you. I don't know what's in them, and I don't want to know. And you don't either."

"So what do I do with them? If the police come back—"

"I already told you," he said, interrupting. "That was completely routine. New regulations went into effect. That's all. If I thought there was any chance the cops were on to you, do you think I'd be standing here talking to you? How dumb would that be?"

"I don't care if it was routine. If somebody doesn't pick up those packages, I'm going to throw them away."

"Don't do that," he said. "Whatever you do, don't do that. These people—you don't want to mess with them." He paused. "Give me a little time. I'll find out what's going on."

He started toward the parking lot and had gone about twenty feet when he turned back. "Don't use this path to get back. Follow the tracks south and find another one."

"Why?"

"Just do it."

"What are you afraid of?"

"I'm not afraid of anything. I'm just careful."

I followed the railroad tracks south just like he said. I didn't find a decent path until I reached the bridge near Sixty-first Street. As I headed down the trail that led back to the street, I saw an old sleeping bag and a jacket and a piece of plastic that was strung up like a tent. I felt as if I'd seen it all before, and then I remembered. The guy I had pushed to the ground: this had been his home.

CHAPTER EIGHT

Sunday morning sunlight came streaming in the little windows of the boat, waking me. It was the first perfectly clear, perfectly sunny day in months. By ten, Golden Gardens Park was filling up with people picnicking, flying kites, lying on the beach.

I walked to Market Street and killed time at Secret Garden books. The only book I've ever bought was the Christmas gift for my dad, but they never chase me out, which is why I like the place. Just before noon, I headed over to the library.

Phrases had been swirling around in my head, phrases I didn't want to think about. *Terrorist cells* and *Red Alerts* and *soft targets*. Arnold had talked about them, and my dad had talked about them, and there was stuff in the newspaper almost every day. I was getting out—but before I got out, I had to know just exactly what it was I'd been in.

I was there when the library doors opened, so I was able to

get a computer with Internet access. I sat down, logged on to Google, and typed in the word *smuggling*. Instantly, the screen filled with websites on the smuggling of drugs and people.

None were what I was looking for.

I went back to the main Google page and typed in what I should have typed from the start: *plastic explosives*.

Immediately the page came alive. I scanned the options, swallowed hard, and opened one. A long article giving the whole history of plastic explosives filled the screen. Some of it I couldn't follow. But not all of it.

Phrases jumped out at me that made me go cold all over. *Easily molded . . . puttylike . . . odorless . . . hard to detect.*

I remembered what my dad had said to me months before. By boat, the Ballard Locks were five minutes from Shilshole marina; the Aurora Bridge was thirty. Ferries and cruise ships were always moving through Puget Sound. Terrorists would have trouble smuggling one hundred pounds of explosives into the country all at one time, but if they got the explosives in little by little, and if they got help from someone who didn't know what was going on—they could succeed.

My head started spinning and the ground seemed to move underneath me the way the *Tiny Dancer* moves in a storm. My breath started coming faster and faster; my hands were gripping the sides of the table so tightly my knuckles were white. I don't know how long I sat there, but when the woman across from me leaned over and asked if I was all right, I snapped out of it.

I let go of the table. "I'm fine," I told the woman. I logged out and left the library.

I had to find a place where I could sit down by myself and think everything through, but the sunny day had brought people out everywhere. Then I remembered Cloud Park on Fifty-eighth Street. It wasn't much more than a bench surrounded by some flowers, but it was close, and it would be empty.

When I reached the park, I sat down, my head still spinning. I had to decide what to do, and I had to decide fast. The obvious thing was to go to the police. But if I did, and if it turned out it wasn't plastic explosives? The cops would have a laugh over that. *Idiot kid turns himself in . . . thinks he's involved in terrorism, when he's just a small-time drug smuggler.*

I could throw the stuff—whatever it was—into the Sound. That would get rid of it, and keep the police out of it. Then I remembered the way the fat guy had looked when I'd said I was going to do that, and I felt fear go through me.

That's when I thought of Melissa. Her dad was a lawyer, a hotshot lawyer, considering the money they had. He'd been my dad's best friend; he'd said he'd wanted to help. To get to him, I'd have to talk to Melissa first.

I fished a couple of quarters out of my pocket and walked over to Walter's. On the wall in the back by the bathrooms were a pay phone and a phone book. I looked up her number, dropped in two quarters, and punched the buttons. The phone rang and her voice came on the answering machine: "No one's home right now. Leave your number and we'll call you. Bye."

I didn't have a number to leave.

When I hung up and turned around, I saw Kim Lawton, my

mom's old friend. "Hey, Chance," she said, smiling. "Good to see you. Have a seat. Let me make you a hot chocolate, or an espresso if you want."

I shook my head. "I can't, Kim. I've got to go."

"Come on, Chance. I never see you anymore. What's the big hurry? Sit down, tell me what you've been doing."

For a moment, I thought of telling her everything. It was eating me up inside, and I wanted to get it out. But what would be the point? She couldn't help me.

"I'll come tomorrow," I said. "Really, I will. But I've got to go now."

"You promise?"

"I promise."

Once outside, I headed down to the marina. I didn't want to go sit on the boat, but where else could I go? I walked down to the water, and then crossed the marina parking lot. Finally I could see Pier B. Then I stopped. Leaning against the chain-link fence was the fat guy. I took a deep breath and then walked up to him. "What did you find out?" I said.

He motioned toward the parking lot. His silver Acura was parked there. "Come on," he said. "Let's go for a ride."

He pulled out of the parking lot and headed along Seaview Avenue. He made the turn toward Sunset Hill, and then drove slowly up Golden Gardens Way, where Melissa lived.

"Gems," he said as he drove. "Sapphires and emeralds and stuff like that. In those red packages. They're from Burma. First they get them across the border and into Thailand, and from Thailand to Canada. Then they smuggle them here. I don't really understand it all. I do know Burma is one messed-up country."

"They don't feel like gems," I said. "The packages are squishy."

"That's an old trick. They hide them inside Spackle or Silly Putty or something like that. Those packages probably still have their labels on them. A customs agent looks at them, and he might not look twice."

"You're sure about this?"

He nodded. "I'm sure. I talked to the main man. I told him I had to know. I told him I was quitting if he didn't come clean."

I looked at the fat guy as he drove. I wondered if he'd been worried about the same thing that had me worried. He eased to a stop at the stop sign at the top of the hill. "This doesn't change anything," I said as he accelerated. "I'm still quitting."

"You told me. OK? You don't have to tell me again. They're going to take the packages off your boat on May first. That's the opening of boating season. There'll be lots of activity on the marina—no one will notice anything. You sit on the bench by the utility building around noon and they'll contact you. You give them the packages and then you're done. Your old man won't be around, will he?"

I shook my head. "Not on opening day. He'll be at the locks looking at all the boats."

"OK then. It's set."

We were back at the marina. The fat guy pulled to a stop; I stepped out of the car and closed the door. As he drove off, I suddenly felt incredibly light and free. I almost wanted to laugh. To think that just a few minutes earlier I'd believed I was involved with al-Qaida and explosives, and all the time the packages had contained gems. Nobody ever got killed by a sapphire.

I spent that afternoon hanging out along the waterfront. The piers were full of people getting their boats in shape for the summer. They'd be going up to the San Juan Islands or to Vancouver Island or Alaska. When people smiled at me or waved or said a few words, I smiled or waved or said a few words back. The sun was out and the whole world looked beautiful.

All the other years I'd lived on the boat, I'd hated seeing the activity at the start of boating season. Knowing that other people were headed off to other places had made me feel nailed to the pier. But now, I felt what they felt. Because I was going, too. As soon as school ended, I was going.

That's when I saw my dad. He was leaning against the railing by Pier K, hollering out advice to some guy who wasn't paying any attention to him. His hair was long again, long and straggly and dirty. His clothes were ratty, and he hadn't shaved in a week.

Maybe the bike shop would end up hiring him, and maybe they wouldn't. It didn't really matter. Eventually, he'd lose the *Tiny Dancer*. It might be three months, it might be three years—but he'd lose it. And when he lost it, he'd have lost everything. He wasn't ever going anywhere on that crummy sailboat. His dream was a kid's dream—like wanting to grow up and be a fireman and rescue babies from burning buildings. Everybody knew that. Everybody but him.

CHAPTER NINE

Tuesday there was a package. Not a red one—there hadn't been any red ones since the night I'd waited on the beach—but one of the regular ones. Still, my hands shook as I shoved it into the backpack. I didn't want to get caught. Not now, not with the end in sight. I turned and headed back to the marina. I wanted to sprint, but I made myself run at my normal pace. Nothing unusual—the same as always. That was the way to act.

As I neared Pier B, I slowed to a walk. A security guard was coming straight toward me. I tried to smile, but felt the muscles in my cheeks twitch. The security guy nodded. "Howdy," he said, dragging the word out like a Texan in a cowboy movie.

"Howdy," I replied, my pronunciation weirdly mimicking his. His smile turned to a glare, but he kept walking.

After I showered, I went back to the *Tiny Dancer*. I had to let my dad know that I was leaving, that he was going to be totally

on his own. I owed him that. I'd told him a couple of times before, but he hadn't really believed me, probably because I hadn't
really believed myself. Now I knew, so he had to know, too.

He didn't show up for an hour, and he'd been drinking.
Still, he wasn't so drunk that I couldn't talk to him.

"I've got to tell you something," I said.

He dropped onto the bench by the wheel. "So tell me."

"It's about June, once I graduate."

"What about it?"

"I'm going to leave here. I'm going out on my own."

He raised his head. "Is that right?"

I nodded.

"OK. What is it you're going to do?"

"I've got a plan."

"How about telling me what it is?"

"Not yet. I will though. And I won't just disappear," I
added, suddenly remembering my mom. "I'll keep in touch. I
promise."

He stared at me, the alcohol haze lifting. "You really mean
it, don't you? You are leaving."

"I mean it."

He looked around the sailboat. "I guess there isn't a helluva
lot for you to stay for, is there?"

I didn't answer.

"Well, good luck and all that." He paused. "I mean that too."

"I know you do," I said.

I started to go down below, but one more thing had to be
said, so I turned back. "You understand what this means,
don't you? Moneywise and all?"

He looked at me. "I understand, Chance."

"You're going to have to—"

He put up his hand to stop me. "I understand."

He left the boat about ten minutes later. I was hoping he'd come back early that night, but around eleven I gave up hoping and switched off the light. I slept until I heard his footsteps overhead, and came completely awake as he made his way into the cabin.

He banged into just about everything as he undressed and climbed into his berth, but once in there, he fell sound asleep within a couple of minutes. I lay in my berth, thinking, as the clock ticked away the minutes. When I probably could have fallen back to sleep, the sirens started. It seemed like a dozen emergency vehicles were tearing down Seaview Avenue. For a second, I thought they were coming after me, but then I figured it was probably some car crash or a fire. A couple of times I thought about going topside to see what was up. Finally the sirens stopped, and a little later I fell asleep.

CHAPTER TEN

At school the next day, I bought a Coke and a package of peanut butter crackers for lunch and sat on the steps just outside the commons. The sun was out, but there was a south wind that made it cold enough so that I had the stairway to myself.

I'd been sitting for about five minutes when the main door opened. I glanced over my shoulder and saw Melissa. "I've been looking for you," she said.

"I didn't think you'd ever want to talk to me again."

She shrugged. "I don't, and I do."

She sat next to me and looked out toward the street. "I got into Brown," she said at last. "The letter came today. My mom just called me on my cell phone and read it to me."

"Isn't that good?"

"It's really good. Some people would say it's even better than Stanford."

"Congratulations. Way to go."

"Thanks."

Somehow she didn't seem happy. "What's wrong, Melissa?"

She shook her head. "I don't know, Chance. It just doesn't seem fair. I'm going off to college and . . ." Her voice trailed off. "You know what I mean."

"Don't worry about me. I'm quitting. A few more weeks and I'm done."

Her eyes brightened. "Swear to God?"

"Swear to God."

For a few minutes we sat watching the cars stop and start on Fifteenth Avenue.

"Are you glad to be finishing up high school?" she asked.

"Sure. Aren't you?"

"I don't know. Sometimes I'm really, really glad to be getting away from here, especially now that I know I'm going to a top school. But there are other times when I think I'm going to miss Lincoln, and I wish I didn't have to leave."

I shook my head. "The only thing I'll miss about high school is you."

As soon as the words were out of my mouth, I wished I could take them back. They sounded so stupid. But Melissa smiled.

"Really?"

"Really."

Just then the warning bell for fifth period sounded. We stood and climbed the stairs, but when I went to open the door, she put her hand on it and turned to me. "Let's write letters to each other next year, Chance," she said. "Real letters.

The way people used to do back in Jane Austen's time. We'll say what's happening inside us, and not just the unimportant things. OK?"

"OK," I said.

"You're not just saying that, are you? You promise?"

"I promise."

I stopped at Walter's after school that day to see Kim Lawton. I'd promised her; besides, now that the days were getting longer, there was no hurry to run out to the rocks.

The place was empty. She made me a mocha, cut me a slice of chocolate cake, and had me sit down at a back table. "So tell me, what's going on in your life?"

"Nothing much," I said.

She frowned. "Come on, Chance. You can do better than that. You're graduating from high school. You must have plans for your future."

"You really want to know?"

"Yes, of course."

"OK then."

Once I started, the words came pouring out. I told her about my plan to enlist in the army, about how it would give me a place to live and a chance to earn some money for later, when I'd really know what I wanted to do with my life. I told her how I had to get away from my dad, from the boat, from Seattle. Everything that I hadn't told my dad, hadn't told Melissa, I told her. It made no sense that I'd open up to her, and I knew it made no sense, but that's what I did.

She sat straight up in her chair, her eyes open wide. "Are

you sure you know what you're doing?" she asked when I finished. "They're killing Americans in the Middle East. You know that, don't you?"

"I know."

"And you'll have to take orders, Chance. Somebody will be bossing you around. *'Do this, do that.'* You've never had that. You don't know what that's like."

Suddenly I wished I hadn't said anything. Because how could I explain to her that I *wanted* somebody to give me orders, that I *wanted* somebody to tell me what to do? Kids like Melissa—they couldn't wait to get out on their own, to make their own decisions. I'd been doing that for a long time, and I was worn out by it.

"I've made up my mind," I said, looking down.

"I'm sorry, Chance. It's just that I knew your mother so well and she's not here now so I'm trying—"

My mother had walked out on me. I didn't want to hear what she would have said. I put up my hand. "Don't, Kim."

"You're right, Chance," she said. "I'll stop; I promise. Not another word."

A customer came in and Kim went to the main counter to help him. I took a bite of the chocolate cake and thought about slipping out while she was busy, but she returned before I had a chance.

"How is it?" she said, gesturing to the cake, her voice cheery, letting me know she wouldn't bring up my mother again or try to talk me out of enlisting.

"It's great," I said, the tone of my voice matching hers. "And so is the mocha."

"Glad to hear it. I made that cake myself, I'll have you know." She pulled up a chair and sat down. "Say, did you hear all those sirens last night?"

"Sure I heard them. They woke me up. Was there a fire?"

"You haven't heard what happened?"

"No."

"Some guy drove his car right off the bluff up at Sunset Hill Park. Right through the chainlink fence."

"Did he die?"

"He sure did. His car flipped about a dozen times before bursting into flames down on the railroad tracks. The cops say it was a suicide." She paused. "Actually, you might know him, Chance. The paper says he worked down on the marina. I've been wondering all day if he ever came in here. If he did, I don't remember him."

She reached over to the neighboring table, grabbed a section of the newspaper that was sitting on a chair, and laid it open in front of me. I took the final bite of cake and looked to where she pointed. Staring at me from the front page was a picture of the fat guy. Only now he had a name: Charles Burdett.

"Did you know him?" Kim asked.

I fought to keep my voice level. "I think I've seen him around."

A group of four women came in. "Got to get back to work," Kim said.

"I should get going, too," I said.

"Come back, Chance. Before you enlist. Come back and say goodbye."

CHAPTER ELEVEN

Sunset Hill Park is a mile or so from Walter's, and the walk is uphill. As I walked, some of the sick feeling left me, but it came back when I reached the park.

The police had blocked off most of it, but even from a distance I could figure out what had happened. Burdett had driven his car across the grass, smashed through the fence at the top of the bluff, and then had taken out trees and bushes as his car flipped down, down, down.

"A strange way to commit suicide, but I suppose it's better than driving head-on into some other car."

Leaning against the fence about ten feet to my right was a tall man wearing a Mariners cap.

"People do that?" I said.

"All the time. Those head-on accidents on the highways—lots of them are suicides. At least this guy had the decency to kill himself and leave the rest of us alone."

"The cops are sure it was suicide?"

The stranger shrugged. "What else? You drive your car forty miles an hour over a cliff, you're not planning on living, are you? It's not like he missed a turn."

I wanted to believe the man, but suicide didn't make sense. Burdett had been nervous, just like I'd been nervous. But he wasn't depressed. He wasn't ready to die. But if it wasn't suicide?

Murder.

The instant the word flashed into my mind, I pushed it out. Murderers shoot people or stab them. They don't drive them off cliffs. How could they? Besides, what did I know about how the fat guy was feeling? Maybe his girlfriend dumped him. Maybe his doctor told him he had cancer. In ninth grade Mrs. LaPonte read us a poem about Richard Cory, a rich factory owner who had everything money could buy but put a bullet in his head anyway.

The man was still looking over the fence.

"What time is it?" I asked.

He glanced at his watch. "Four-forty."

"Thanks," I said, and then I headed down to the marina.

I wasn't sure what to do. The smugglers would read the newspapers; they'd find out what happened. With Burdett dead, there was a ninety-nine percent chance the smuggling would stop—at least for a while. That meant I could stop, too. But then I remembered the warnings Burdett had given me. If a package was hidden in the rocks, and I didn't bring it to the locker, they—whoever they were—might think I'd stolen it, and come after me. Besides, if nothing was hidden, what did it matter if I ran along the beach and poked around in the rocks below the railroad tracks? I was just a high school kid out jogging—nothing illegal about that.

So I ran, just like I always did, out to the locks and then back along the beach. When I reached the tree, I stopped, stretched, and then searched the rocks.

Nothing. Just like I expected. I breathed a big sigh of relief, turned, and started to run back along the beach. That's when I saw them.

There were two of them, and they were standing on the boardwalk that cuts between the two duck ponds and leads from the parking lot to the beach. They were wearing sport coats, slacks, and hard shoes—not clothes that anybody wears on the beach. They seemed to be staring at me, though the sunglasses made it hard to be sure. I jogged past them, and then turned and ran backwards a while so that I could look at them again. They were still there, and they were still watching me.

Clouds had rolled in, covering the sun, and a strong wind was blowing from the south, so I picked up my pace a little. A few kite fliers were on the grassy field; a few beachcombers walked along the water. No one was at the Teen Center; Little Coney's was empty. Even the fancy restaurants seemed deserted.

I ran along the marina until I reached Pier B. I grabbed a change of clothes from the boat and then went to the utility room. I unlocked the door, pushed it open, walked back around the corner to the shower stalls, and undressed. I held my hand under the water and fiddled with the shower nozzles until I had the temperature just right.

I stepped in, closed my eyes, and let the hot water stream

through my hair and down my body. After that, I soaped up and washed myself head to foot. I washed as if I hadn't bathed in months.

I was rinsing the soap off when I heard the main door open and then slowly click shut. My heart started pounding. What had I been thinking, coming in here? I'd been a fool. A total fool. I'd cornered myself. They were going to murder me just like they'd murdered Burdett. I'd made it simple for them.

I looked around for something to fight with, but there was nothing. Desperate, I grabbed the shampoo bottle. I left the water running, and silently stepped out of the shower. I tied a towel around my waist, and then flattened myself against the wall and slowly edged my way to the corner. My only chance was to surprise them.

I held the shampoo bottle as if it were a rock. I was going to throw it at the nearest guy, throw it with all my might, and then make a dash for the main door. If I got through the door and out onto the parking lot, I'd start screaming, "Help! Police!" When the cops came I'd tell them everything, even if it did mean I'd go to jail.

I took a few shallow breaths to steady my nerves, gripped the shampoo bottle tightly, and then stepped out into the main locker room, ready to fling the bottle with all my might at the men and then run, run for the door. But instead of two murderers, a little boy was standing at the sink rinsing off a green plastic bucket and a bright red plastic shovel.

"Hi," he said, looking over at me.

I lowered the shampoo bottle.

"Hi," I answered.

CHAPTER TWELVE

I grabbed my clothes from my locker, returned to the shower area, and dressed. While I was dressing, the little kid slipped out. Before I left, I flicked off the overhead light, slowly cracked open the utility room door, and peered out. Nothing—no black Mercedes, no guys in sport coats. I stepped onto the sidewalk, pulled the door shut behind me, and quickly hurried to the ramp leading to Pier B. I opened the gate and pulled it shut behind me. For the first time in my life, I looked closely at it. It was solid metal and was at least fifteen feet high. If someone were coming after me, they'd need a ladder to climb over it or a sledgehammer to break it down, and they couldn't use either without a lot of people hearing them or seeing them.

Back on the sailboat, I climbed down into the cabin and sat at the navigation table. I had to think it through. I had to take my time and think it through.

Burdett had told me that the smugglers were going to contact me. I *wanted* them to contact me. So why was I getting panicky about the men on the beach? The police were undoubtedly going through Burdett's files and papers and stuff. Maybe the smugglers were afraid the cops would find something that would blow the whole scheme. Maybe they wanted to speed up the transfer. That would be OK with me. What I had to do was stay cool and wait. If they contacted me early, I'd give them the packages and I'd be done with it. If they didn't, I'd turn the stuff over on May 1. Either way, everything would work out, just so long as I didn't panic.

But there was another possibility. If Burdett hadn't killed himself, if he'd been murdered, then once these guys got what they wanted, they might murder me too. It was a paranoid, crazy thought—but no matter how hard I tried, I couldn't shake free of it.

I had to talk to somebody. I was in over my head—way over my head. But who? The only friend I had was Melissa, and I couldn't go to her. For a second I actually thought about calling Mr. Arnold, but that was impossible. Who else was there? I sat, my hands shaking. Who? Finally I grabbed a jacket, zipped it up to my chin, stuck on a baseball cap, and set out.

The Sloop Tavern is about half a mile from Pier B. When I reached it, I tried to peer in, but the windows are tinted and the front door was closed tight. I put my shoulder to the door, pushed it open, and stepped inside. Not much to see: a pool table, a couple of pinball machines, a dartboard, a television tuned to a Mariners game, the volume down. At the bar, three guys were talking quietly, glasses of beer in front of them, blue cigarette smoke curling above their heads.

I looked to the booths. Two of them were empty, but someone was sitting at the farthest one, his back to me. I started toward him. "Hey, kid, you've got to be twenty-one to come in here," the bartender said, stepping out from behind the bar.

"I'm looking for my dad," I said, walking quickly toward the back booth as I talked. "Jack Taylor. You know him?"

The bartender blocked me. "Sure I know him. Everybody knows Jack. But he's not here. Hasn't been here all day. And you're going to leave right now. I'm not losing my license for anybody."

I was certain the bartender was lying, that it was my dad sitting in that booth, but just then the man turned toward me. He was no more than twenty-five years old, but he had the bloated red face and bleary eyes of a drunk. Our eyes caught, and then the guy looked away.

The bartender stepped toward me, forcing me back. "I'm going," I said, turning. "Don't worry."

"I'm not worried," he said, but he stayed right with me until I was out the door.

There are probably a dozen taverns along Ballard Avenue. If my dad wasn't at the Sloop, I figured he had to be in one of them. So I kept walking, looking through windows and sticking my head through the doors of place after place. But even if he was drinking in one of those taverns, my chances of finding him were slim. When it started to rain—a cold, steady rain—I headed back to the boat.

Along Market Street, just past the locks and before the marina, there's a deserted stretch of road. No businesses, no houses. As I walked those blocks, I had a feeling I was being watched. More than a feeling. A certainty. I kept looking over my shoulder, but no one was there. Even when I came out of that dead stretch and into the bustle of the marina, the feeling didn't go away.

I turned down the blue ramp leading to Pier B. At the security gate my hands were shaking so much I fumbled with the key a couple of times. Finally I managed to open the gate. I walked down the pier and was just about to step onto the *Tiny Dancer* when, through one of the cabin windows, I saw the back of someone's head—someone I didn't recognize.

He couldn't be a murderer. He just couldn't be. No murderer would walk down the pier on a busy afternoon and sit in our cabin, his head visible through the window.

But he was one of the smugglers. Who else could he be? I'd been right—Burdett's suicide had speeded up the timing. The man was on the boat to get the packages—that was it, that had to be it. All I had to do was go onboard and hand them over. He'd take them, and I'd be done with everything forever.

I stepped quietly onto the boat, my mouth dry with fear. The deck looked strange, and for an instant I couldn't figure why. Then it hit me. Everything was clean. The benches, the little table, the deck—all of them were shining and clean. There were no ashtrays filled with cigarettes, no beer bottles or newspapers stuffed into the trash can.

From down below I heard a cough. I maneuvered past the

wheel to the steps leading down to the cabin. I grabbed hold of the companionway railing and took one step down. "Hello," I said, "I'm coming down."

It took a moment for my eyes to adjust. The man had a sponge in his hand and was wiping down the table. He was wearing a white shirt and slacks, was clean-shaven, and had short, gray-black hair.

CHAPTER THIRTEEN

"**H**ow do I look?" my dad said as he ran his hand over his smooth chin.

It took a while before I could answer. "You look good, Dad. But what's going on?"

"I got a job, Chance. A real job. Medical benefits, dental benefits, sick days, vacation time." He looked at his watch. "In fact, I start in an hour. That girlfriend of yours. Melissa. Her father and me were good friends in high school. But you know that, don't you?"

"You called Melissa's father?" I said.

"No, he called the marina office and they came and got me. It's nothing special. I'm a janitor at his office building downtown, that's all. Nights and Saturdays. I'll mop the floors and empty the trash. Not exactly what I had in mind for myself when I was your age, but it'll keep me going once you're gone and on your own." He paused. "And that brings me to something else. Isn't it about time you told me just what it is you're going to do once you graduate?"

I looked at him with his clean clothes, his clean hair, his clean face and hands, his new job. "I'm going to enlist," I said.

"In what?" he said.

"The army, just like you did. I got a brochure at school a couple of months ago. It makes sense for me."

He nodded. "I guess it does. I just wish all this stuff wasn't going on in the Middle East."

"So do I," I said.

"They'll give you money for college when you get out. Use it for college. You hear me? Don't get some pretty girl pregnant and end up married before you're ready."

"Is that what happened with you and Mom?"

"That's what happened. I don't mean that I wish you weren't born, Chance. I only mean—" He paused, then started again. "I only mean that I don't want you to end up like me."

I wish I'd said something then, something about how he was OK by me, but I didn't.

He looked at his watch again. "I got to go. I can't be late my first day." He smiled. "Maybe on day two, but not the first day."

He turned to leave. "Can I ask you something?" I said.

"What?"

"Why'd you get kicked out of the service?"

He laughed. "Drinking, fighting, missing curfews. Nothing big, but string together a whole bunch of stupid little things and you can do yourself in."

"But you didn't ever run away in battle, or anything like that?"

The smile disappeared. "Is that what you thought? No, Chance, I never ran away. I was a good soldier under fire. It was the other times I had trouble with."

After he left, I realized I hadn't told him about Burdett and the packages and the guys in the sport coats on the boardwalk by the duck pond. But that was OK. In fact, I couldn't remember why I'd ever wanted to tell him. After all, what could he do for me? What could anyone do for me? I'd gotten into this by myself; I'd have to get out of it the same way.

CHAPTER FOURTEEN

The pickup would happen on Saturday, May 1, which was just two weeks away. Normally two weeks is nothing, here and gone. But nothing was normal anymore.

I told myself over and over that I was being stupid. The police had said Burdett killed himself. It was idiotic to think that he'd been murdered, idiotic to think that somebody might murder me. But it didn't matter what I told myself—inside I was scared. Every stranger on the sidewalk, every car on the street, became a threat. The slightest noise in the night and I'd instantly be wide awake, wondering, *Is it them? Are they coming for me?*

I kept to a strict routine. I left for school at the same time every morning, returned to the sailboat at the same time every afternoon. I ran out to the locks, across the Magnolia footbridge, and then back to the drop-off spot by the maple tree. I poked around in the rocks, and then ran back to the *Tiny*

Dancer. If someone was watching me, I wanted them to see that I was doing everything exactly the way I had always done it, the way I'd been told to do it. I wanted them to know I was reliable, that they could trust me to turn over the packages to them.

Day after day after day I stuck to the same schedule, but as May 1 grew closer, my head started to ache and my blood was pumping so fast I could hear it drumming in my ears. I just wanted Saturday to come; I just wanted those packages off the boat.

On the Friday morning before May 1, I couldn't stop looking at the clock during my classes. I didn't know seconds and minutes could take so long to pass. Fourth period ended at eleven-forty-five, but already I felt as if I'd been at school for a week. I ate, or tried to eat, my lunch in the commons. But when the bell sounded for fifth period, I just couldn't face it. Instead of going to class, I went out the gym door and headed back to the boat.

It was strange walking down to the marina at that time of day. Fewer cars were on the streets, and everything seemed quieter. When I crossed Thirty-second Avenue, it was as if I was the last person in the world. The only sound was the occasional bark of a dog. It was actually a relief to hear a car coming up the street behind me.

Or it was a relief for a few seconds. But then that feeling turned to fear. The car was going too slow—it should have passed me by now. Instead it was inching along behind me. I wanted to turn and look, but I was afraid to. I told myself to count to ten, and then, if the car hadn't passed me, then

I'd turn and look. I started counting. . . . *One . . . two . . . three . . . four . . .*

I turned at *eight.* Forty yards behind me was a black Mercedes. As soon as I turned, the driver accelerated and the car flew by me, tires squealing as it rounded the corner and turned onto Seaview Avenue. It was the same car I'd seen that time I'd come out of the utility room; I was sure of it.

My mind started clicking like a railroad car moving down the line. I'd been right. They had been watching me, all the time, and I'd just done the stupidest thing I could possibly have done—I'd changed my routine. For seven months I'd come home from school at the same time. And now, the day before the pickup, now I was early. The one thing I didn't want them to think was the only thing they would think—that I was changing things on them, that they couldn't trust me. I'd blown it. Right at the end, when I'd needed to play it cool, I'd blown it.

That's when I thought of my dad. He wouldn't be at work, not now, not in the middle of the afternoon. He'd be sitting on the boat, not knowing anything about anything.

I was almost running by the time I reached the parking lot in front of Pier B, and I did run when I reached the ramp. I was fumbling for my gate key when a guy who owned a new Catalina a couple of slips down from ours pushed the door open from the inside. I stepped by him onto the pier. It was that simple—the security gate wouldn't stop anybody.

I hurried down the pier, my eyes on the *Tiny Dancer.* It looked so small, so very small, and so peaceful in the still water. A boat like any other boat, and all of what I feared seemed like a dream. But those red packages were real; the black Mercedes was real; the death of Burdett was real.

The boat wasn't a terrible mess topside, but someone had been there, looking. The garbage can was tipped over. The bench seats were in the upright position; the sweaters and blankets stored beneath them were tossed about. I swallowed hard, then made my way to the steps leading into the cabin.

That's where the real mess was. The icebox, the shelves, the drawers—everything had been tossed around like so much trash. Cans of food rolled around in a puddle of milk mixed with orange juice. The mattress and pillows in the sleeping berths had been slit open.

I climbed into my own berth, pushed the ruined bedding aside, and crawled forward. I hoped that they'd found the secret storage nook, found it and taken the packages, and that it was all over. But even before I slid the panel open, I knew they hadn't. And I was right—they were still there: a dozen red packages lined up side by side. I'd hidden them too well. I closed my eyes and slumped down onto the mattress. That's when I heard footsteps overhead and—a moment later—my father's voice. "You want to tell me what's going on?"

CHAPTER FIFTEEN

I told him everything, beginning with Burdett following me into the utility room back in October and ending with the black Mercedes racing past me that afternoon. It took about ten minutes. During that time, he never interrupted and he never acted surprised. It was as if I were telling him things he already knew. And I guess in a way I was. All along he'd suspected I was doing something illegal.

"And you think the guys in the Mercedes tore up the boat looking for those packages?"

"I don't know who else it could have been."

After that, neither of us said anything for a while. Then he opened up his pocketknife and motioned toward my berth. "Grab one of those packages, Chance. We might as well find out what they're smuggling."

"I told you," I said. "There are gems hidden in them. Emeralds and stuff like that."

"So let's take a look. I've never held a real emerald in my hand."

I picked up one of the packages and handed it to him. He carefully slit it open. Underneath the red packing paper was a layer of wax paper. He peeled it away. Underneath that was a doughy substance. "And you think gems are hidden inside this stuff?"

"That's what they told me."

He pulled it apart, poked his fingers through it, but found nothing. He held it to his nose and smelled it. Finally he put it down and stared at it.

He was just about to say something when we heard a rattling at the security gate. We both looked at each other. He motioned for me to stay still, and then he climbed up and looked. When he came back down, he shook his head. "Just Kovich leaving."

We both looked back to the doughy stuff on the table. "It's some kind of plastic explosive, isn't it?" I said.

His eyebrows went up. "How do you know about plastic explosives?"

"Is that what it is?"

He nodded. "In the army I once handled some stuff called Semtex. It was a lot like this. A lot like this."

We both stared at it, trying to take in what it all meant. It didn't seem possible. Not me. Not my dad. Not Shilshole marina. Not the *Tiny Dancer*. Something like this couldn't happen here, to us. And yet, there it was. I looked toward the other packages. "How much damage could all this do?" I asked.

"None, without a detonator. And I don't see one here. But hook up a couple of wires and a battery—" He stopped and shook his head.

"We've got to call the police."

"Be quiet, Chance," he said. "I need to think."

"What's there to think about? We've got to get out of here right now and call the police. They're sure to come back. If they killed Burdett, they'd kill us too."

His eyes fired with anger. "I said I need to think. OK?"

I sat still, my heart drumming in my chest, while his eyes seemed focused on something very far away. Finally he spoke. "Listen to me, Chance, and listen carefully. You know Kovich's inflatable boat?"

"What does that have to do with anything? Dad, we have to get out of here."

"Just answer me. Do you know the boat?"

Kovich owned the sailboat moored in the slip next to us. A little yellow inflatable was always tied to the stern. "Of course I know it."

"All right. Here's what you're going to do. You're going to slip onto his boat and then onto that inflatable. Once you're on it, you'll row to the beach, ditch the inflatable, and then go straight to Trevor Watts. I want you to tell him everything you've told me."

"Melissa's father? Why him? Why not the police?"

"Because the police won't believe you, not without checking it out for themselves. If the cops come down here now, the men behind this will know it's over and just slip away. That's why."

"I don't care if they get away. I just want to get off this boat and go to a phone booth so we can call the police. I'll tell them everything. I don't even care if I end up in jail. It's what I deserve, anyway."

My dad shook his head. "You're not thinking, Chance. These are terrorists we're dealing with. Terrorists. If they get away now, they won't stop. In six months or a year they'll have a new target, a new plan to blow something up and kill somebody or thousands of somebodies. I'm not going to let that happen. You think of me as a bum. I know you do, and I don't blame you, because that's all you've ever seen. But I told you I was a good soldier, and I was. I was very good. I'm going to get these guys, Chance. But I need your help. I need you to get to Trevor Watts. So will you do it? For me?"

CHAPTER SIXTEEN

My father went topside first. I followed, and he screened me as I edged my way along the starboard side of our boat to a place where I could slip onto Kovich's boat. Once aboard, it was simple enough to get into the inflatable. It was so low in the water, and there were so many other boats around, if someone were looking for me, they'd have had trouble seeing me.

I rowed past the line of piers till I cleared the breakwater and was in Puget Sound. The wind was in my face, slowing me, but I only had to row a couple of hundred yards to reach the beach. I made it in just a few minutes. The wind actually helped me row up onto the sand. I grabbed the inflatable, pulled it off the beach, and left it hidden in the scrubby grass by the dunes.

I made my way across the parking lot to the stairway that led to the Blue Note Café. I went straight up, fast, turning to look every twenty steps or so to see if I was being followed. No one.

When I reached the top, I checked my watch. Two-thirty. Melissa might not be back from school yet. I stood for a second, unsure what to do. Maybe her father was home; maybe he'd let me in. Maybe he'd listen to me. Maybe he'd believe me. Maybe, maybe, maybe. Why had I ever told my dad I wouldn't go to the police? It was such a stupid promise.

But I'd made it. I'd made it and I'd stick to it. I turned north and headed along Golden Gardens Avenue toward Melissa's house. At first I ran, but then I realized that I wasn't sure which house was hers. I remembered that it was brick and that it sat at the top of a winding driveway, and I thought I remembered a security gate at the bottom of the driveway, but I wasn't certain.

I walked quickly along the west side of the street, craning my neck up at the homes above me. The first had white siding; the next was brick, but it seemed too new and too small. The third was all glass and windows. I felt panic coming on.

"Chance? What are you doing here?"

I turned, startled. The voice had come from across the street. Melissa was stopped, engine idling, her head leaning out the window, confusion on her face.

I ran across the street and quickly got into the passenger seat next to her. "I've got to talk to your father," I said. "It's an emergency."

She smiled. "My father? What? Are you going to ask for my hand in marriage?"

"This is no joke, Melissa. The stuff I've been smuggling— some of it wasn't drugs, some of it was explosives. All of it is stored on the *Tiny Dancer*. My dad is on the boat right now.

He's in danger. The smugglers—they're terrorists. They've searched the boat once already looking for the stuff; they're sure to come back. They're killers, Melissa. They're killers."

The smile disappeared. "You're serious, aren't you?"

"Melissa, I need to talk to your father right now."

She shook her head. "I don't get it. Why my father?"

"Because that's what my dad wants me to do. He trusts your father." I paused. "Please, Melissa, we're wasting time. If you know where your father is, you've got to take me to him now."

She pulled into traffic. "He's home, Chance. Or at least he should be. He promised to take the afternoon off to buy me a new laptop for college."

CHAPTER SEVENTEEN

Less than a minute later she pulled the Jetta into her garage. We both climbed out and she led me through a back door into her house. "Let me talk to him first," she said. "Explain things."

"No," I said, "I've—"

"Let me talk to him, Chance. I know him. It'll be faster." She saw the impatience in my eyes. "Trust me. Go through that room to the stairway. At the top, turn right. You'll see the solarium. Wait there."

She disappeared through a door. I went where she pointed, walking through a huge room with sofas and bookcases and Oriental carpets and paintings. A fire was going and classical music was playing even though no one was there. I found the stairs and climbed them to the solarium, which turned out to be a large sunroom with granite floors, a big-screen television, and ceiling fans to circulate the air.

A telescope was mounted on a tripod in a corner. I tilted it downward so that I could look through the viewfinder toward the beach. The blurry specks that had been people were suddenly so clear I could see the moles on their faces. I thought about how hard I'd tried to make sure no one saw me poking around in the rocks. What an idiot I'd been! All of the homes along the bluff had telescopes on their decks, binoculars in the cabinets. People lived here because they loved looking at the beach, the mountains, the sky. How many of them had trained telescopes or binoculars on me?

I swung the telescope around toward Pier B. I wasn't sure if I could pick out the *Tiny Dancer,* but it was worth a try. I scanned down the piers slowly . . . Pier G, Pier E, Pier C, and finally Pier B. I checked out the ramp and the security gate. Everything looked completely normal. I slowly moved the telescope from boat to boat. There was lots of activity; people who hadn't been on the pier in months were getting their boats ready for opening day. Dozens of sailboats were out in Puget Sound, where a week earlier there had been fewer than ten.

I moved the telescope slowly down the pier, hoping to see my dad. A couple of times I scanned too fast and the telescope jumped way off line. Finally I managed just the right touch.

There was Tasker's sailboat with the Mariners windsock, then Nelson's at slip 41, Heller's at 43, and after that Kovich's boat. I stopped—somehow I'd jumped over the *Tiny Dancer.* I ran the telescope back. Kovich's boat, then Heller's, then Nelson's. One more time, with my heart pounding: Nelson's boat, Heller's, Kovich's.

The *Tiny Dancer* was gone.

Just then I heard footsteps coming up the stairs, moving fast. I stepped away from the telescope as Melissa's father came through the door.

I'd pictured him as tall and thin with glasses and maybe a trim beard or a goatee. Instead he was a balding, barrel-chested little guy. "Think for a minute, Chance. Then tell me exactly what I need to know right now. OK?"

His voice was calm, but intense. His eyes were intense, too. Whatever Melissa had said had had its effect. There was no doubt in his expression—he was ready to act.

I left out any explanation of how the explosives got on the *Tiny Dancer*, and just told him what was there. "There's something else," I said, gesturing toward the telescope. "The *Tiny Dancer* is gone."

"Did your father tell you he was going to take it out?"

"No, and he wouldn't have unless he had to. It hasn't been out in years. The rigging, the sails, the hardware—it's not seaworthy."

"What are you thinking, then?"

"That he took it out into the Sound to keep the terrorists from getting to the explosives. Either that or . . ." I couldn't bring myself to say it.

"Or what, Chance?" Mr. Watts said.

"The terrorists have got the boat."

CHAPTER EIGHTEEN

Mr. Watts turned and headed downstairs. Melissa and I followed, and then waited as he made a series of phone calls. I couldn't tell who he called, but I thought it was the Coast Guard and the police, and maybe the FBI. Every once in a while he'd turn and ask me a question. "What was the slip number? . . . The length of the sailboat? . . . Any distinctive markings?" Finally he hung up. "Let's go," he said.

"Where?" I asked.

"There's a police helicopter waiting for us down on Lake Union. Chance, your dad might be out there by himself, safe as can be, but we can't make that assumption. If terrorists have hijacked the boat, then it's a floating bomb. There are a hundred, no . . . a thousand, different targets out on the Sound. We've got to find the *Tiny Dancer* before any of those targets get hit."

"I'm coming too," Melissa said. "And don't tell me I'm not."

"You are coming," he answered. "In fact, you're driving. I'm expecting some phone calls."

We hurried out to the garage. I climbed into the back seat of the Jetta and her father took the passenger seat. Melissa backed the car out, whipped the wheel around, and maneuvered down the driveway and out onto the street. "Drive fast," her father said, "but not too fast. No accidents. You got it?"

The police helicopter pad on Lake Union is about five miles from Melissa's house. Instead of taking the neighborhood streets, she drove through the Ballard industrial area that runs right along the water. The roads are potholed and crisscrossed by abandoned railroad tracks, but there are few lights or stop signs.

As we passed under the Ballard Bridge, her father's cell phone rang. The person on the other end spoke for a few moments. "Are you asking me what I would recommend?" he said.

The caller said something I couldn't hear.

"OK," Melissa's dad answered. "Here's what I'd do. I'd close every single bridge over the water. I-5, I-90, Aurora, 520—all of them. And I'd hold every ferry at the dock."

Again the caller spoke.

"I know it would paralyze the city," Melissa's father said, his voice angry. "And I know this is a long shot. But better to paralyze the city than to have a whole bunch of people dead."

He snapped the phone shut and slipped it into his pocket.

"Are they going to close the bridges?" I asked.

He just looked out the window.

We were nearing Gas Works Park. "Up there," he said to

Melissa. "That gravel road. Turn right and drive all the way to the end."

Melissa followed his directions. As soon as the Jetta came to a stop, we got out, and three men ran up to us. "Is this the kid?" one of them said, pointing to me.

"That's him," Melissa's dad said.

"You come with me," the man said, and he grabbed me by the arm and led me toward a stairway.

"What about us?" Melissa called after him.

"Just the boy," the man said, waving her off.

Before I had a chance to object, we were headed up the stairs. At the top a helicopter, its blades whirring, sat on the pad. "Keep your head down," the man said. "Now move."

We ran, his hand grasping my upper arm, to the helicopter and I climbed onboard. It was the first time I'd ever been near a helicopter, and the sound of the blades was about twenty times louder than I'd expected. I sat in a cushioned seat and fastened my seat belt just as the copter lifted off. Another man handed me a pair of binoculars. "You know how to use these?" he shouted.

I nodded.

"All right then. Find that sailboat for us."

CHAPTER NINETEEN

The helicopter rose off the pad and headed east toward Lake Union and the major bridges. It was the wrong way and I knew it. There hadn't been enough time for the *Tiny Dancer* to sail into Lake Washington. The boat would be in the cut or still out on Puget Sound. "We should be going west," I shouted to the man.

"Just look," he said, pointing to my binoculars. So I looked. White sails dotted the lake, powerboats cutting between them. The copter flew low toward the I-5 Bridge.

"See anything?" the man shouted.

I shook my head. "They couldn't have gotten here," I said again. "There hasn't been enough time. We need to go west."

"Are you sure?" he said.

"I'm sure."

The man shouted to the pilot. The pilot looked at me.

"West," I yelled. "West." The pilot shrugged, then turned the copter around and headed west.

I kept remembering what my dad had said about the Ballard Locks. Was that the terrorists' target? On a sunny day like this, there would be hundreds of people leaning over the railing watching the boats pass through, and more people onboard the boats tied side by side in the locks.

Finally we were over the locks. The sailboats were so close to one another that it was impossible to read the names. We hovered overhead; people pointed skyward, puzzled and excited by our presence. Once I thought I saw my father, but then two little boys wearing orange life preservers came on deck and waved to me.

"Anything?" the man shouted.

"No," I shouted back.

"You sure? We could stay longer."

"I'm sure."

The copter rose in the air and headed out over Puget Sound.

CHAPTER TWENTY

've lived near the Sound my whole life, so I know it's big. But I'd never realized how big until that moment. The pilot shouted something to the man sitting next to me, who turned to me. "Which direction?"

Which direction? I had no idea. It would be a guess, nothing more. And if I guessed wrong? Then it came to me. South led to the city of Olympia and land. North led to the Strait of Juan de Fuca and out into the Pacific Ocean. That's where my dad would go.

"North," I shouted to the man. "Head north." He nodded and the copter banked right. Within a minute we were over Shilshole marina. I raised the binoculars to my eyes and looked down.

Police cars blocked off the entire marina; a line of fire trucks clogged the street in front. SWAT team members were walking up and down Pier B. The whole thing was unreal; it couldn't be happening, but it was.

I felt a nudge. "Look for the boat, kid."

That brought me back. The man would point, and I'd focus the binoculars on sailboat after sailboat. "No. No. No." It was hopeless. Hopeless and pointless. Those old guys who comb the beach with their metal detectors hoping to find a diamond ring had a better chance of finding what they were looking for than we did. Puget Sound was too big; the *Tiny Dancer* was too little.

The radio crackled. I couldn't make out much of what the pilot was saying, but I could pick up the excitement in his voice. "What is it?" I said to the man next to me. "What's happened?"

"There's a boat sailing erratically. It passed right under the prow of a freighter, and now it's headed north in the wrong traffic lane."

"My dad wouldn't do that."

"He might if he's trying to attract attention."

The helicopter dipped and then headed northwest toward Kingston. Below and ahead, I could see a patrol boat racing in the same direction as we were. The men in the boat were armed with rifles. "There!" This time it was the pilot shouting and pointing. "There!"

My hands were trembling so much from cold and from fear that it was hard to bring the binoculars into focus on the boat. But finally I did. Standing at the wheel of the sailboat was my dad. "That's him!" I shouted. "That's my dad!"

A strange calm came over me. It was all going to be OK.

Nothing had happened, and nothing would happen. The Coast Guard or the port police or whoever was in the power-boat below us would intercept the *Tiny Dancer*. They'd capture the terrorists, my dad would be fine, and nobody would get hurt. If I ended up in jail, that would be OK. Just as long as nothing terrible happened.

The copter pilot nudged the man next to me and then looked north. I followed his eyes and saw the *Norwegian Sky*, a huge luxury liner that carries at least a thousand passengers, and the calm that had filled me dissolved. The *Norwegian Sky* was less than half a mile from the *Tiny Dancer*, and the two vessels were on a collision course.

"What's your dad doing?" the man next to me shouted.

I looked back to the *Tiny Dancer*. My dad had left the wheel and he was taking in all the sail. Two men were on the deck pointing guns at him. I could tell they were screaming at him and that he was ignoring them.

Suddenly, I understood. My dad had seen the *Norwegian Sky*. He wasn't going to let terrorists use the *Tiny Dancer* to blow it up. He'd die first.

The rest happened fast. The patrol boat pulled up about one hundred yards from the *Tiny Dancer*. I could see someone shouting into a bullhorn while two other men pointed rifles. A gunshot was fired from the *Tiny Dancer* toward the patrol boat. Right then my dad jumped one of the men. As the two of them scuffled on the deck, the other man clambered below. My father grabbed the man he was fighting, spun him around, and hit him hard in the stomach and then again in the face. The man reeled backward and fell off the boat into the Sound. My dad picked up the man's gun from the deck. He waved it over his head in the direction of the helicopter. I'd put the binoculars down, but I could still see his face clearly, and I think he could see me. He smiled, and he looked happier than I'd ever seen him. Then he turned and started down into the cabin after the other guy.

That's when the *Tiny Dancer* exploded.

CHAPTER TWENTY-ONE

The helicopter had turned and was flying back toward Lake Union. The blades were whirring; the pilot and the man next to me were shouting at each other; the walkie-talkie radio was alive. I heard it all, and I heard none of it. A numbness came over me, a numbness of mind and body. The *Tiny Dancer* was a ball of flame. My father was dead.

After the helicopter landed, two tall men wearing sunglasses led me to a beige Chrysler. Melissa's father forced himself into the back seat of the car with me. "I'm his attorney," he said to the men. "Wherever you're taking him, I'm going."

As we drove off, I saw Melissa standing by her Jetta. She waved to her father, and he rolled down the window. "Go home," he said as the car drove quickly away. "I'll be there later."

Twenty minutes later I was sitting alone in a room on the thirty-eighth floor of an office building in downtown Seattle.

Mr. Watts was in a separate room; I could see him through a glass window talking to a balding man in a gray suit. The two talked for ten or fifteen minutes. They could have kept talking forever, for all I cared.

When Mr. Watts finally came out, he sat down next to me. "Chance, did you know you were working for terrorists?" he asked, his voice low.

"No," I said.

"You're sure."

"I'm sure."

"All right, then. Here's what I want you to do. I want you to answer every question you're asked, fully and completely. You understand what I'm saying?"

I nodded.

Mr. Watts motioned to the man in the gray suit. He came over, showing me his badge as he spoke. "My name is Don Benjamin. I work for the FBI. I'm very sorry about what happened to your father. Very sorry. We all are. I know you must be in a state of shock and I wish I could give you some time. But there are questions you have to answer, and you have to answer them right now. You understand that, don't you?"

"I understand," I said. "Ask whatever you want. I'll tell you everything I know."

Hours later, Don Benjamin turned off the tape recorder and tapped his pencil on the desk. "That's it for today, Chance. We'll need to speak with you again, though. OK?"

I nodded. "OK."

Mr. Watts led me out of the room and we took the elevator

down. "Are you hungry?" he asked as the elevator went down and down and down.

"Not really," I answered.

"We're going to eat anyway."

There was a Starbucks in the lobby. He ordered a coffee and a sandwich for himself, and he bought me an apple juice and a muffin. We sat at a table away from everyone else. I was able to drink the apple juice, but looking at the muffin made me want to throw up.

Neither of us spoke for a long time, but finally I couldn't keep the words in. "I killed him," I said, looking down at the table. "I killed him."

Mr. Watts shook his head. "Don't do this to yourself, Chance. You didn't know what was going to happen. How could you? Nobody did."

"I killed him," I repeated.

For a while he didn't say anything. Then he took a deep breath and sighed. "Listen to me, Chance. I knew your dad. We both knew him. He didn't want to be a janitor mopping floors at night. He wanted more than that from his life. He expected more than that from his life. Today, he got it. He's a hero—you know that, don't you? He stopped a terrorist attack. He saved people's lives. Lots of people. Your father died the way he wanted to die. It's a rare person who manages that. A rare person."

I picked up the fork and turned it back and forth. I knew what Mr. Watts was trying to do—he was trying to take some of the guilt away. Most of what he said was true, and I knew that too. My dad was no janitor. The look on his face that last time I saw him—I'd never seen him look like that. But it was what Mr. Watts didn't say that ate at me, and that eats at me still. My dad died a hero on the *Tiny Dancer,* and I'll always be proud of him. Always. But that I put him there—that's my shame. And that shame will be with me my whole life.

I put the fork down. "Can we go now?" I said.

Mr. Watts stood up. "I'll get us a taxi."

CHAPTER TWENTY-TWO

One week has passed since the explosion. Since then, I've spent every day answering questions. Sometimes it's the FBI asking, sometimes it's Homeland Security, sometimes the port police or the Seattle police. Once it was the Royal Canadian Mounted Police. Mr. Watts is always with me, but there's nothing that anybody asks that I don't answer. I'm not hiding anything; I'll answer questions for as long as they want to ask.

The FBI found the black Mercedes in the Shilshole marina parking lot. Inside were a bunch of maps of Puget Sound and of Seattle. The Ballard Locks, the Aurora Bridge, the ferry routes—all of them were circled in red. But so were the Space Needle and Safeco Field and the University of Washington, so nobody is really sure what they were trying to blow up. Mr. Watts says they probably didn't care, that they just wanted to blow up something and kill a lot of people. But the only person they killed, beside themselves, was my dad.

There was a memorial service for my dad three nights ago. A huge crowd of people filled Phinney Ridge Lutheran Church. I sat in the front row with Melissa and her father and mother. As people filed in, I couldn't keep myself from looking around, hoping to see my own mother. She must have heard what had happened; it had been in the newspapers and on television. I had a small hope that she might actually be in the church, be close to me, but be afraid to talk to me. I wanted her to know that it was all right, that she could talk to me, that I didn't hate her. Once in a while, I'd catch a glimpse of a woman who looked something like my mother, and my heart would start to pound, and then I'd look closer and see it wasn't her.

I was glad when a female minister finally stepped to the podium and said a prayer. After she finished, men I didn't know spoke about how good a soldier my father had been in Kuwait, and how he had died a soldier and a hero. Melissa cried and her mother cried and even Mr. Watts cried. Around us complete strangers cried. But I didn't. Even after all the speeches at the memorial service, even after seeing the coffin with the American flag draped over it, I didn't cry. I don't know why I didn't, but I didn't.

I've been staying at Melissa's house all this time. When her father suggested I move in that first night, I told him no. "Where else can you stay?" he asked, and I didn't have an answer. I sleep in a guest bedroom that's bigger than the *Tiny Dancer*.

Yesterday the FBI was done with me at three o'clock, which was earlier than they've ever been done with me before. The questioning was finally coming to an end, though one agent told me they might be talking to me off and on for years to come.

"When are they going to arrest me?" I asked Melissa's dad once we were alone.

"What?" he said.

"When are they going to arrest me?" I repeated. "I know I broke the law; I know I helped terrorists; I know I'm going to jail."

He shook his head. "I've worked it out with Mr. Benjamin. As long as you cooperate, nobody is going to arrest you. You were a pawn in all this; the FBI knows that and so do the police. Your father died a hero. His picture was on the front page of all newspapers around the world. There's no way the government is going to put you in prison."

"But you don't understand, Mr. Watts," I said. "I have to go to jail. I have to make up for what I did."

He folded his hands in front of him and leaned forward. "You're right, Chance. You do have to make up for what you've done. But serving time is not the only way to do that. And it's not close to being the best way."

"Then what is the best way?"

He shook his head. "You'll have to find that out for yourself."

He drove me to his house and dropped me off. "I've got to get in to work," he said. "Someone will probably be home. If not, there's a key under the mat. Just let yourself in."

I walked up the long driveway and knocked on the door. Melissa answered. I'd been sleeping in her house for a week, but this was the first time I'd been alone with her. She hugged me, and I held her close. Then she led me by the hand into her living room and had me sit down next to her on the sofa. For a while, neither of us said anything. It was almost as if we didn't know each other.

"What are you going to do now, Chance?"

"What do you mean?" I said.

"I mean when all this settles down. What are you going to do?"

"I guess I'll finish the school year somehow," I said. "After that, I really don't know."

"Listen. I've got it all figured out. I've already talked to my mom and dad about this, and they are one hundred percent behind it."

"Behind what, Melissa?"

"They want you to stay here, with us, indefinitely."

"Melissa—"

"Hear me out," she said. "My brothers are both away at college. They only come home for a week now and then, and you can see how big our house is. I'll be gone in the fall, so my mom and dad aren't worried that we're going to become secret lovers or anything like that. You could go to Shoreline Community College. My parents will pay the tuition. After a couple of years, you could transfer to the University of Washington or wherever you want to go."

I shook my head. "I can't do that, Melissa."

"Why not?"

"I just can't."

"At least think about it, OK? Do that much."

□   □   □

After dinner, her mother and father took me out into the living room and said basically the same things to me, only in a different way. "Your father and I were best friends once," Melissa's dad said. "He'd look after Melissa if anything happened to me. You know he would. So let me look after you."

I started to object, but Melissa's mother gently put her hand over my mouth. "Don't say anything now, Chance," she said softly. "Think about it. Think about it for as long as you want. Everything has been happening so fast. There's no hurry at all."

I spent most of last night wide awake, staring at the ceiling. Melissa's parents meant every word they said; I knew that. They wanted me to stay. And it made sense, in a fairy-tale sort of way. They would take me into their magic house and make me a part of their magic family. I could go to college, maybe become a lawyer, be like a third son to them. They would give me Thanksgivings and Christmases and birthdays, and they wouldn't even notice all that they were giving me. It was just the way they lived.

But that was what stopped me. It was the way *they* lived. It wasn't the way *I* lived. If I moved into Melissa's house, their life would become my life. The *Tiny Dancer,* my dad, my mom—all that had happened might become unreal—like a story a stranger tells you about something that happened to someone else. But it hadn't happened to someone else—it had happened to me. It was my life—both good and bad—and nothing was going to take it away from me.

I cried for my dad then. For the first time ever, I cried for him. Because rocking back and forth on a boat headed nowhere wasn't the life he'd wanted. Now he was dead, and he'd never get to live that life. I don't know whether the drinking took it from him, or whether he drank because his life had gotten away from him. I'll never know, just like I'll never know why my mother hasn't come back to be with me, not even now, with my dad dead. But I do know my life isn't getting away from me.

It's just before seven in the morning. I'm sitting in Melissa's solarium looking out over Puget Sound. The sunlight is on the Olympic Mountains; some early sailors are out on the water. I can hear Melissa downstairs talking to her mother and father. They're probably talking about me.

In a few minutes I'll have to tell them. After that, I'll go to the bus stop and take the number 75 out to Northgate and enlist in the army.

Maybe enlisting is a big mistake, just like Melissa and her parents and Kim Lawton and everyone else thinks. Maybe it isn't. In a way it doesn't matter. Because if it is a mistake, when the time comes I'll do something else. One thing I'm sure of—I am going somewhere someday. I'm going for myself, and I'm going for my dad, too.